I0624574

Origins of a Fetish

Experiences: Book 1

The Evolving Fantasies and Fetishes of a Gentleman

Simone Freier

OTK Publications
www.OTKPublications.com

Origins of a Fetish

EXPERIENCES: BOOK 1

By Simone Freier

Published by OTK Publications
http://otkpublications.com

Copyright © 2014-2016 OTK Publications
All rights reserved

ISBN: 978-1-942054-00-9
Third Edition

Manufactured in the United States of America

COVER DESIGN BY OTK PUBLICATIONS

Caution: This work contains mature content, including graphic sexual descriptions and scenes, and is provided for adults only. Neither the author nor the publisher intends to encourage or promote any of the activities depicted in this work. Many of the specific activities and scenarios described in this work can potentially be dangerous, and should not be attempted without special knowledge or training and, as appropriate, use of sterile single-use supplies. No information contained herein is intended to constitute advice or serve as instructional material, and this work should not be relied upon to ensure safe practices in real life.

Table of Contents

CHAPTER 1: HENK & ZÖE

The doorbell rang, and I glanced at Sarah, "I guess Henk and his friend have arrived." We walked from the kitchen where we were cooking a special Indonesian 'reistaffel' for our guests. It was a bit crazy attempting to prepare a meal that they could have eaten in dozens of restaurants in their hometown of Utrecht, but we enjoyed cooking ... and challenges. Our reistaffel would consist of only about a dozen dishes, far less than the 20-30 delicacies that one would find in a typical Dutch Indonesian restaurant. We would not be serving it over flames and grouped by the 'heat' of the dishes, as is common in The Netherlands, but we *were* using fresh spices that we had ground this morning.

We opened the door, and greeted our guests. "Henk! Welcome to the states, and to our home!" Henk was tall – well over six feet – and thin, with longish brown hair that fell in a disheveled bang over his forehead. He wore jeans and a dress shirt; blushed cheeks and a perennial smile distinguished his oval face.

Henk shook my hand vigorously, "Sam it's good to see you again – this time on your own turf." Then he turned to Sarah, bending down to kiss her three times, alternating cheeks, and handed her a wrapped package. "Hello Sarah, thanks for inviting us to visit." When Sarah glanced down at the package, Henk commented, "Just a few Dutch treats."

Henk then turned to his friend, "And this is Zöe. She's come to the states before, but has only seen New York."

As Zöe handed Sara a bouquet of flowers, I took note of her features: She was also tall, although several inches shorter than Henk, and wore jeans and a knit sweater, appropriate for our winter weather. Zöe had shoulder-length sandy blond hair, and incredibly blue eyes – almost mesmerizing in their clarity. She was a full-figured woman – not quite 'Rubenesque', but her sweater did not hide the fact that she was big on top. Zöe also had a nice smile, but my eyes kept returning to those incredible eyes. She appeared to be wearing no makeup.

Sarah kissed her three times, following the usual custom, and then it was my turn. "I'm glad you could visit, Zöe. I think you'll find this area a bit more relaxed than New York! Come on inside, and we'll get some coffee to warm you up."

I brought Henk and Zöe into the living room, and we sat around the coffee table, as Sarah brought a tray with coffee and an assortment of cookies. She told them, "It's not Dutch coffee, but I think you'll enjoy it: One hundred percent Blue Mauka from Kona, in Hawaii." She poured steaming cups and passed them around.

Henk laughed, "Well, now you've got some real Dutch coffee, and I also included a small tin of 'stroopwafels' – little round sweets that look like waffles and have caramel in the center. We usually put them on top of the coffee mugs, where the steam softens them. I don't know if you tried them when you visited me last year."

Sarah shook her head. She had accompanied me on a business trip, and Henk had taken us to dinner in Utrecht. It had been quite exotic, an African restaurant located on one of Utrecht's many canals. After visiting Amsterdam, Utrecht and Rotterdam, we had driven to the south of

Holland, over the 'dyke project' – finally complete after decades of construction. I had visited a research lab in Eindhoven, before continuing down to Maastricht, where we stayed at a health spa in the Valkenburg area.

Henk turned to Zöe, "Sam and I work at the same pharmaceutical company; he's in charge of international research. I'm the regional product manager for the newest drug that his team developed." Then Henk looked at me, "Sam, are you still planning to retire this year? We're going to miss you."

I nodded, "Yes. It's time for some younger blood to take the helm." Henk sipped his coffee, so I continued the explanation of our backgrounds to Zöe. "Sarah works at an ad agency, and also travels a lot – mainly to New York and London, where her company has branches. We're hoping to travel together more in the future, without it always being about business. There are a lot of places in the world that we'd like to visit." I took a sip of coffee and asked, "So what do you do, Zöe?"

Zöe smiled, "Well, I'm not as high-powered as you guys. I work for a company that rents apartments all over Holland; I mainly find short-term rentals for people vacationing or on business in Amsterdam."

Sarah's eyes lit up, "We loved Amsterdam: The Rijksmuseum, Van Gogh Museum, Stedelijk modern art museum, Rembrandt's house ... and Ann Frank's house; and performances at the Concertgebouw. We mostly did the tourist stuff. Just walking along the canals is beautiful."

Zöe was nodding, "Yes, there's a lot of history and art in Amsterdam. But there are too many tourists. And, most think of Holland as a wild place, due to all the coffee shops where you can buy marijuana, the red light district with women in the windows, and all of the sex shops."

Henk was laughing again, "Yeah, most tourists don't realize that we're a very conservative and religious country – at least outside of the big cities."

I had to break in, "But the Dutch are very open and tolerant people. They seem to accept everyone, regardless of their looks – for example, tattoos or crazy hair colors – or their moral views."

Henk looked at the ceiling, and then back to me, "Yes, the Dutch are tolerant. We have had a mix of ethnic cultures since the great trading days of the sailing ships. Now, a sizeable percentage of the population is Indonesian, Surinamese, Caribbean, Turkish, Moroccan, and Chinese. But I'm not sure what you mean by 'open'?"

I explained, "Well, for example, lots of Dutch people visit the saunas," I turned toward Sarah, "like that place – Thermae 2000 – where we stayed when we drove to the south. Most Americans wouldn't think of going to a 'mixed' sauna, where everyone changes in the same locker room, and walks around nude all day in front of dozens of strangers ... and maybe their neighbors."

Henk laughed, "I guess that's true. But that's how we are raised. When I entered university, our 'fraternity' – which had both men and women – had a 'get to know each other' event the first week, where we all went to a sauna. There was a little modesty, for the first few minutes. But everyone soon forgot about their bodies and just had a good time. Most Europeans don't put much significance on nudity, certainly not like the Brits or Americans."

Zöe perked up, "That's what we need right now, in this weather. I wouldn't call it cold, compared to home, but a sauna would be great. You don't have any in this town?"

Now, it was my turn to smile, "Well, there are no public mixed saunas, like you're used to ... but, actually, we have a sauna right here in the house. Why don't we show you guys around, and then I'll help Henk bring in your suitcases, and we'll get you settled?"

We got up, and I grabbed a couple of cookies as I led everyone to the kitchen. "We're making an Indonesian dinner tonight, which I hope you'll like." I pointed out the breakfast area, and then took everyone out to the backyard.

Zöe's crystal blue eyes widened, "This is all yours? We would have to be out in the country to get this much land, and it would cost a fortune!"

We walked around the black-bottom pool and jacuzzi, and along a winding path under some large trees, now barren of leaves. "It's too bad you're seeing it in the winter; we usually have lots of flowers, and our lawn is much greener in the summer."

After the partial tour, Henk and I went out to his rental car, and brought in the suitcases; then, we continued the tour upstairs. Sarah said, "Here's your bedroom, and the bath is across the hall. I've stocked it with towels, but please let me know, if you need anything else." We dropped the suitcases in the guest room, and finished the tour in the master bedroom.

Again, Zöe was impressed, "Look at the size of this closet! No wonder our American clients always complain, when I show them an apartment in Amsterdam! At least, the women. And the men usually complain about the price: Amsterdam is getting pretty expensive. We have some really great properties, with a canal view, for only $6000 per month."

Sarah whined, "That's too bad. I was hoping you could find us something for our next holiday. But that's a little over our price range."

Zöe pointed out, "That comes out to only $200 per night, about the same as a 2-star hotel. But it only makes sense if you're going to be staying there a while."

We went back downstairs, and continued down to the basement. Henk whistled, "You've got a big place, here."

I explained, "Yes, there's a lot of potential, but we haven't finished the basement, only this bathroom." We turned into the bathroom, which looked normal with a sink and toilet – until we turned the next corner. "We have a great shower area, with rain shower, jets for your legs, and a small seating area for relaxing after the sauna." I pointed to the smoked glass door, set into the wood-paneled wall, "And here's the sauna."

Zöe opened the door and peeked in, "This is nice. It's plenty big enough for four people. And it's hot, already." I had wanted to be prepared, and had a feeling that we might want to use the sauna today, as it was too cold to enjoy the backyard.

Sarah reached into the narrow closet between the toilet room and the shower room, and handed Henk and Zöe two terrycloth robes. "Why don't you guys get unpacked and settled, and then you can put these on, and we'll continue our conversation in the sauna, if you like?"

———————————————————

Twenty minutes later, we all met back downstairs. Sarah and I had already showered, and were in our own robes, lying back in the chaises, reminiscing about our sauna experiences in Europe. Henk and Zöe walked into the shower room, casually took off their robes, hanging them on hooks next to my chaise, and stepped into the shower. I explained, "The large knob on top is for the rain shower; you can set the temperature, but it's already set for warm. The lower knobs are for the jets that can be aimed to your legs. The center knob has another temperature dial for those jets."

We watched as Henk and Zöe turned the large knob, and huge drops of water fell from the ceiling, like a heavy tropical rain. Sarah and I took off and hung our robes, and grabbed towels on the narrow shelf. She pointed, "You guys can take large towels from this shelf. We'll meet you in the sauna." Then, we opened the glass door, and slipped into the cave-like environment that had a predominant cedar aroma. The heater was already set to 185 degrees Fahrenheit, and the sauna was nearly up to that temperature.

Sarah and I placed our towels on the top bench, letting them drape down the wood, and onto the lower bench, where we put our feet. I thought again how most Americans would not know to do this, although it was considered basic hygienic practice throughout Europe. I smiled at Sarah, "I figured they would want to go in the sauna, and assumed we would do that this evening. But maybe it's better now, before we've all had too much wine."

Sarah nodded, "It's too bad we can't go in the pool, but at least the jacuzzi is heated, in case we want to use it between our saunas." That was a good idea. At least it would give us a change of scenery.

As we waited for our guests, I thought how good Sarah looked at 40: She had D-cup breasts, but was otherwise quite petite, with an athletic and well-toned body, having gone to the gym and done short runs for the past decade. Although I had loved her long dark hair when we met, she now sported a more conservative short hairstyle. She had never waxed down below, and still had a full 'bush' of dark hair. I leaned over and kissed her. We were deeply in love, and had been since we had met more than two decades ago.

Henk and Zöe walked into the sauna and, after allowing their eyes to adapt to the dark, they climbed up and sat next to us on the L-shaped top bench, arranging their towels as we had done, so that no part of their body was directly contacting the wood benches. I stepped down and used a wooden ladle to pour some water from an old-fashioned wooden bucket onto the rocks in the sauna heater, releasing a billowing cloud of steam that instantly made the sauna feel hotter.

We sat on the bench, everyone acclimatizing to the new environment. Henk sat next to Sarah, while Zöe sat on the L portion of the bench. Henk was in his mid-30's and looked quite fit, most likely from all of the 'football' (soccer to us Americans) that he played. I remembered that he was also an avid bicycle racer, which explained the taut muscles of his long legs. Small droplets of sweat were already appearing on his firm chest; he would be perfectly suited to appear in a commercial for one of those 'ab' machines.

Zöe was more rounded, with large breasts and hips, and only slightly smaller waist, which gave her a 'solid' physique. Her blue eyes appeared black in the dim red light of the sauna. She looked around the sauna, and said, "This is really a professional sauna. How nice to have it in your house; just like they have in Finland."

I laughed, "Well, a lot of the Finns have sauna cabins outside, using wood-fired heaters. At least we don't have to walk through the snow to get to our sauna!"

We were all quiet for the next couple of minutes, as our bodies heated up, droplets of sweat now glistening on all of us. I reached over and ran a finger over Sarah's nipples, causing large drops of sweat to fall to her thighs. She smiled at me.

Zöe looked at us and asked, "I guess, as Henk told me, you guys aren't the typical Americans?"

That provided a good opening for us to explain some of our views. "Hardly. We've been going to nude beaches – what you call 'naturiste' – for almost 25 years. We grew up in the late 1970's – the tail end of the hippie era – and were always quite liberal. On our honeymoon, we visited an island off the coast of southern France that was a naturiste resort."

Sarah explained, "I know it's nothing for you guys, in this day and age, but back then it was pretty shocking to a couple of American kids."

I continued, "We each bought a 'kepi' – little triangles of cloth with three strings attached, basically a G-string – and followed the beach trail, hiking along the spectacular coastline. Just before reaching the beach, we came upon a clearing with a sign (in French) that said, 'Enjoy the beautiful water and air ... but do it our way, without clothes'. Sarah and I just shrugged and took off our clothes. We put on the kepis, as that is what we thought we should do."

Sarah picked up the story, "But when we got to the beach, everyone was totally nude, and we soon felt self-conscious wearing the kepis, and they quickly came off. As we sat there, looking around at all the nude people, we made a few remarks about some girls who were getting sunburned bottoms – thinking that nobody around us would speak English. However, the gentleman next to us looked over, smiled, and said, 'Yes, you do need to be careful in this sun!' He turned out to be a world-famous cellist, who came to the island frequently."

Then I continued, "We went into the water ... Sarah at the depth where her breasts were bobbing on the surface, when I told her, 'Well, at least there's nobody from the U.S. here'. At that moment, a Brooklyn-New York accent came at us from behind: 'Get in! The water's great!' So we made another friend, and soon became very comfortable being nude around other people."

Sarah said, "We tried introducing several of our friends back home to nude beaches, but most of them were too uptight. However, over the past 20 years, we have brought many people to nude beaches – or swimming holes for skinny-dipping, and they have all enjoyed it."

Zöe nodded, "As Henk said, it's normal for us, and nobody thinks about it." She looked down, and ran her hands along her body to wipe off the streams of sweat. "Were you guys part of the hippie 'free sex' scene that I've read about?"

Sarah and I looked at each other, and she nodded imperceptibly. I looked at Henk, and said, "Henk, since we're business colleagues, I normally wouldn't share this kind of thing with you ... but as I'm going to retire soon, I will trust you to keep what we say private until then."

Henk nodded, "Of course. We all have our 'little secrets'. But you know that we Dutch are very direct – I guess what you would call 'open'; probably as much as you Americans. It would be interesting to hear about your experiences."

I am an open and honest person, but was concerned this might be taking it too far. I decided to open up to Henk and Zöe and see how they would react to some of our stories. "Well, as I said, we were both very liberal. We were in college at the end of the hippie era, and I always fancied myself as a hippie."

Sarah broke in, "Yeah, Sam, the scientist, wanted to be a hippie. But that was never going to happen. His values are very different from those that were typical of the hippies."

I let that slide. "Anyway, we got married young, and weren't very sexually experienced. But we're quick learners. We even participated – briefly – in the wife-swapping and group-sex scenes. We already understood by that time that being nude doesn't compromise our relationship: Others can see us nude and we lose nothing. Similarly, we found out that even having sex with others doesn't change our relationship, or feelings for each other. Eventually, the novelty wore off, and by the early-1980s the AIDS epidemic was well publicized and extremely scary. My pharmaceutical exposure taught me about HPV, herpes and other sexually transmitted diseases ... some of which are incurable. This, and the possibility of pregnancy, eliminated our interest in having sex with other people."

Henk nodded, "That makes sense. You guys were very young then; lots of couples experiment with sex. Until they realize that there may be consequences. But you could have used condoms ..."

"Henk, you know that condoms may be 95% effective, but they're not perfect. When we were facing an incurable deadly disease, we didn't want to take that chance, however small." Henk just shrugged. "And although Sarah wasn't interested in going after other guys, she was still open to me 'playing' with women friends – as long as I didn't have sex with them."

Sarah added, "I even told Sam he could have sex with other women, but 'just don't come back and expect to have sex with me!'" She chuckled.

I nodded, and explained, "As we had a good sex life with each other, that was definite enough for me not to want sex with other women." Now, I decided that if we had gone this far, I should explain what we considered 'sex'. While this may seem to be an easy question, it has been the subject of presidential hearings.

I took a deep breath and began. "We do not have any particular 'moral' feelings about sex. However, there are the practical considerations: Will the woman get pregnant? Will either of the partners contract a deadly disease? And, will either of the partners become emotionally involved, to the exclusion of his/her spouse?"

It was getting hot, and I knew we wouldn't be able to stay in the sauna much longer. So I finished up this part of the discussion quickly. "After we had kids, I had a vasectomy, so getting a woman pregnant was not a consideration. The emotional aspect could be difficult, but if both partners are just looking to 'play', that should be manageable. Finally, a big issue was catching a sexually transmitted disease. As I said, condoms have a finite chance of not working. So the only really safe way to prevent STDs is by eliminating all possibility of fluid contact."

Zöe asked, "What does that mean?"

I explained, "This definition of sex is quite precise. It precludes genital-genital, genital-anal, anal-anal (how do you do that?), oral-genital, oral-anal ... and, yes, even oral-oral contact. So kissing would be considered 'sex'. In fact, by this definition, even eating or drinking after each other would be considered sex! This may be too strict a definition for some people, but it is entirely practical. And, when you think about it, this definition allows EVERYTHING ELSE to be a possibility! There are a lot of things two people can do to have fun together that do not involve fluid contact." I smiled, "However, I would admit that most people (both men and women) do not have the self-control to have such a relationship."

Zöe said, "I'm ready to cool off for a while."

We all agreed, and stepped out of the sauna, hanging up our towels, and getting into the shower. We stood close together under the rain shower, which was set on cool, and I turned on the leg jets and set them even cooler. After a quick rinse, we put our towels around us, and I suggested that we go out on the patio to cool off even faster.

We sat around the patio table, and I was surprised that Henk prompted me to continue the discussion. "So have you guys actually taken advantage of your unique definition of sex?"

I nodded, "I have been fortunate in experiencing openness and trust from a wide range of my female friends. From sharing a room together during a trip, to camping with each other, and giving massages; from peeing in front of each other, to showering together. All without having any ulterior motive, except to have fun, and enjoy the wonders of being with a partner. Actually, females tend to be much more in-touch with their bodies, more open to nudity, and more accepting of bodily functions than are most men. Inhibitions primarily arise from a religious or moral background but, fortunately, have usually faded by the time a mature age is reached."

I continued, "On the other hand, it is amazing how many people cannot separate the meanings of SEX, LOVE, and NUDITY. There can certainly be nudity without sex or love. There can be love without sex or nudity. There can be sex without love ... and even sex without nudity (as we found in the case of one of my wife's great-aunts, who had never let her husband see her nude, but had several kids, presumably by her husband). If one can separate these concepts clearly in one's mind, then many possibilities become apparent. One of the greatest Christian fears is that nudity would lead to sex. Sex is viewed as intended for procreation, rather than for enjoyment, and the thought of sex without love is considered unwholesome ... but it certainly happens all the time.

"It is only necessary to have a 'mature' attitude towards the body, sexuality, and friendship. And find a partner who you can trust, and who will trust you – to play, and even have sexual fulfillment, without having 'sex' per our definition of fluid contact. Once these ideas solidified, we felt a freedom we had not enjoyed since our single days: We could have relationships, 'play' with other people, and do exciting things, without fearing reprisal, without danger of pregnancy or disease, and without doing it in secret from our spouse. That would only be the seed for a destroyed relationship. However, being able to share experiences with others – and being trusted by your spouse to have those experiences without endangering her/him – make them even more exciting and satisfying."

Zöe commented, "I think most younger people in Europe have this 'mature' attitude that you speak of. Men and women may be more comfortable with each other at home, than they are here in the states. Almost every woman uses birth control, so pregnancy is not an issue. We don't worry as much as Americans about STDs, if we're dating people in our same socioeconomic class, and using condoms. So what you're describing may be mostly an American phenomenon."

I agreed, "Yes, we grew up here in the Victorian tradition of modesty, innocence, and abstinence. For a while, our government was preaching to teens 'just say no to sex'; but, obviously, that is extremely unrealistic. However, if sex education classes taught what could be done without having intercourse, I think a lot of young – and older – people would be happy to have such a relationship. A friend. A playmate. A way to have 'sex' without commitment, danger, or expectation. Having fun, and exploring new experiences."

Zöe asked, "Can we go in the jacuzzi?"

I laughed, "Of course. Sorry for the long-winded discourse." We stood up and unwrapped ourselves, leaving the towels on our chairs, as we walked over to the jacuzzi. The cold air was just beginning to seep into our skin and chill us.

Zöe stepped into the jacuzzi, and said "Oh! This feels really good!"

I turned on the pump for the jets, and water from the spa cascaded down the rock waterfall and into the pool. We were all enjoying the feeling of the water and bubbles on our backs. Zöe was against the edge of the jacuzzi, looking over the steep drop to the pool, slightly moving herself up and down; I realized that she was using one of the jets to stimulate her lower parts. I couldn't resist. "Zöe, are you open enough to allow me to help you?"

Zöe looked at me, and said "What?" Then, her face reddened, and she said, "I don't think so. Henk probably would not like that." Henk just shrugged.

I laughed, and said, "OK. I was just testing your limits." Of course, had she said, 'yes', I would have snuggled behind her, putting my arms around her, holding her breasts, and then letting them drop beneath the water, down to her genitals; stroking her labia, and positioning her for direct stimulation of her clit by the jets. Or, letting her sit in my 'lap', as I reached around and fingered her clit. But Henk was a business colleague, and it would not have been 'appropriate', even given the discussion we'd had, and the fact that we were all nude, already.

Instead, I decided to push in a different direction. "So what kinds of things turn you guys on? What are some of your fantasies?"

Henk coughed, and quickly said, "Sam, I'm not sure I can share that with you. At least, until you're retired, and we're not working together." He looked at Zöe, and said, "But perhaps Zöe would like to share some of her turn-ons?"

Zöe gave Henk a 'look', and he nodded and shrugged. Zöe turned around to face us, her back against the wall of the spa. She closed her eyes, and then opened them, the lakes of dazzling blue piercing through the atmosphere between us. "Well, actually, I'm bi. I love playing with men and women; sometimes separately, and sometimes together."

Sarah blinked, and I heard a sharp intake of breath. "Ooooh." Then she recovered, and added, "That sounds like fun."

I knew that Sarah had experimented a couple of times with other females when we were in college, and we had played around with 'group' sex early in our marriage. Well, not exactly sex, but group touching, massaging, and stimulating – in every combination of males and females. But she had never agreed to any of my suggestions to try a ménage a trois. I briefly wondered whether Henk and Zöe's visit could change that; but I was probably getting my hopes up too much. Fortunately, nothing else was 'getting up', and I put these thoughts out of my mind.

Henk was obviously anticipating our thoughts when he commented, "I'm quite open to Zöe doing whatever she likes. A few times, she has brought home another woman; occasionally I've been allowed to watch, but I'm almost never invited to participate with them."

Zöe reasoned, "Well, maybe that's because most of the girls I've brought home are not bi; they're gay. They're not interested in having a man involved."

At that, Henk stepped out of the jacuzzi, and walked toward the deep end of the pool. I had to warn him, "Henk! The pool is not heated. It's really cold!"

Henk looked at me and smiled, then turned and dived into the frigid water. He swam towards the jacuzzi underwater, and then broke the surface, breathing heavily, and running his hands through his hair. As he treaded water, he said, "all saunas have a 'cold pool'; yours is just larger than most. It feels exhilarating."

I bet it did. I was getting cold just watching him. It only took another minute before Henk was ready to get out of the pool; he walked to the patio table, grabbed his towel and exclaimed, "I think I'm ready for the next sauna course, now."

We all laughed, and got out of the jacuzzi, taking our towels, and following Henk down the stairs to the sauna. After a quick rinse-off under the shower, we went back into the sauna, again arranging our towels, and sitting on the upper bench. After a few minutes of quiet, Henk looked over at me and asked, "So what are your fantasies?"

I had asked for it. I wasn't too concerned about our work relationship, only about what our guests would think. These things were difficult to explain. Sarah gave me a 'you've gotten yourself into this' look – which I often got from her, when pushing social situations like I had done today. Both Henk and Zöe were looking at me; waiting for my response. Could I do this?

"Well, I guess I'll be the 'direct American' and share some ideas with you. But I'm not sure I can fully explain them without telling you about some experiences in my past that have contributed to my fantasies."

Henk and Zöe were listening, and kept their eyes on me, prodding me to continue. I glanced at Sarah, who promptly said, "Don't look at me! You're on your own." I guess I was.

I started slowly, "Well, there are two things that really turn me on. And they can be summarized as … submission." I had done it. Now, I just had to explain.

Zöe said, "You mean BDSM." It wasn't a question. I realized I would have to be more specific in my categorization, before I told them some of the incidents that had molded my thought processes.

"Not really. Well, maybe. It depends on what you think those letters mean. I'm not interested in bondage (although I wouldn't mind trying some Shibari with someone who was into that). I enjoy seeing a female voluntarily submitting ... to some pain; but I'm not a sadist: I don't really want to hurt anyone, I just want to see them submit. It doesn't have to be physical pain, as I'll explain in a few minutes. And I'm not interested in the girl being a masochist; if she wants the pain, then she is not submitting."

I took a deep breath, "As far as dominance, I guess that is part of it, if someone submits; I'm not turned on by my dominance, but by someone else's submission." I wiped the sweat from my brow, wondering whether it was from just the heat of the sauna. I looked at Henk and Zöe and pleaded, "Let me tell you a couple of stories, some of my memories of childhood, and early adulthood. The stories that I believe, at least in part, led to my current fantasies."

Henk and Zöe nodded, and Zöe sat cross-legged on the L-portion of the bench, while Henk moved down to the lower bench, spread his towel, and lay down – his head on a wooden triangle provided for that purpose. They seemed very relaxed. I was glad that we were able to share the sauna with them. But I wasn't sure yet about sharing the stories I was about to tell.

CHAPTER 2: CHILDHOOD MEMORIES

The girl looked up at her instructor and said, "Yes sir, I was smoking. I know it was wrong. I'm sorry, I won't do it again." The instructor just looked at her, and eventually said, "Ann, you know what this means." The girl looked down at the ground, and quietly murmured, "Yes, Sir." The instructor commanded, "Fetch the cane." The girl walked across the classroom to a cabinet on the back wall, opened it, and took out a 36" bamboo cane. She brought it back to the instructor, and held it up in both open hands. He took the cane, and said, "Take your position." The girl bent over the desk, and her hands went back to lift up her skirt and petticoat, revealing her white cotton underwear. She felt like she was about to faint, realizing what was about to happen, but was lucid enough to think, 'I'm glad this school doesn't allow bare-bottom canings for girls!' The instructor took his position behind, and slightly to the side of the girl, placed the cane on her quivering buttocks, pulled the cane back and, with a whoosh, it cracked across the poor girl's bottom. She let out an involuntary shriek, but held firmly onto the desk. She knew that if she stood up, or brought her hands back to shield the blows, the caning would be started over. Six strokes were administered, carefully, but brutally, the girl sobbing, tears freely flowing, by the time the sound of the last stroke had died out. She was shaking, but realized that her punishment had been deserved. She was glad that she hadn't been expelled, or had to face her own father's belt, back in the woodshed. The instructor told the girl to arrange her skirt, compose herself, and go to her next class. The girl, still in tears, stood up, flipped her skirt down and smoothed it. She wiped her eyes with a handkerchief, and looked up at her stern instructor, "Thank you sir. It won't happen again." He smiled, and said, "Go along, young lady!"

"I must have been about 10 years old, at home with the flu, watching an old black-and-white movie on television. It was a movie from the 1930's, and showed a way of life that was totally foreign to me. This was the early-1970's;

men had already traveled to the moon! And here, a girl was voluntarily complying with her teacher, staying in position and not complaining, while he thrashed her backside with a cane! It was unbelievable."

I laughed, "OK, I exaggerated: The girl on television did not bend over the desk and lift up her skirt – as usually portrayed in Internet images and videos of schoolgirl spankings. Actually, after presenting the cane to the instructor, the girl held out her hands, palms up, closed her eyes, and kept still, as the instructor delivered a stroke of the cane on each hand. The girl was in tears, but cooperated fully with the instructor in taking her punishment.

"It wasn't until my high school days, on the gymnastic team, that I witnessed – and experienced – school-based corporal punishment. Nearly every day, at the beginning of the workout, the coach would call out someone who had done something inappropriate, and he would have to go to the front of the gym, bend over and hold his knees, and take one or two incredibly hard swats – with a ½" thick wooden paddle that was at least 18" long.

"This also seemed unbelievable to me, but I was older now, and realized that not taking the punishment would be grounds for expulsion from the team. And, for many of the guys, it was a show of strength to disobey, and then not display any reaction to receiving swats from the coach.

"In my senior year, something very strange happened: A girl joined our gymnastics team! In those days, there was still strict segregation of the genders, with separate boys' and girls' gyms, gym classes, and teams. The girl was a great gymnast, as strong as most of the boys, and was accepted surprisingly quickly onto the team. It was an incredible turn-on, when she misbehaved somehow, and had to go to the front, bend over, and take swats from the coach! This evidently had been a condition of joining the team – that she would be treated just like the boys.

"I eventually earned a swat by working out without a matt under me, early in the morning. The one swat was a stinger, and I felt it for at least 2 hours after I left the gym. It was not a turn on at the time, but gave me a glimpse of what it would be like to be on the receiving end, and hold your position, knowing that you were in store for pain.

"In the very early days of our marriage, we played some games with another couple, that included spanking. In one of them, the guys played pool, and after running a series of balls, the other guy's wife had to bend over the pool table, and receive a spanking from the guy who made the shots. After each rack, the women would have to remove one more piece of their clothing. The women cooperated well, but it wasn't much of a turn-on for me. We weren't spanking hard – it was just in play – and the women were laughing. It was more of an act than any kind of real punishment or submission."

I looked over at Sarah again, "Sarah and I have tried a few spanking sessions together, but they were never as exciting as in my fantasies – perhaps because we knew we trusted each other, and wouldn't hurt each other badly. Unfortunately, as I grew more interested in spanking, Sarah became less interested. If I wanted these experiences I would need to look elsewhere. But I've never gone to a club or looked for someone else to 'play' with."

I was really getting hot. "Would you guys like to cool down? I'll get some ice water for all of us, so we don't get dehydrated. We can sit on the chaises, and I'll continue the story there. If you still want me to."

Everybody agreed, and we exited the sauna. I rinsed and dried off quickly, and went upstairs to the kitchen to get a pitcher of water and glasses with ice. I returned with a tray that I sat down on the small round table between the chaises. Sarah was sitting on a chaise, and Henk and Zöe were having fun in the shower, re-aiming the leg jets, adjusting the temperature, and generally frolicking about.

I sat down next to Sara, sideways on the chaise, and she asked me, "Are you practicing your 'openness' today?" I grimaced; perhaps I shouldn't have gone so far. But now that I had released half the cat out of the bag, I might as well let the other half out. I wasn't sure which half was the head or the tail.

Henk and Zöe turned the shower off, and I suggested, "Put your towels in the hamper. You can take a fresh towel for the chaise, and two more for yourselves." Henk put on his robe, leaving it open in the front, and lay back on the chaise. Zöe spread a towel across the bottom of the chaise, and sat cross-legged, pushing Henk's feet off the chaise and onto the floor. Henk was now straddling the chaise, his robe falling open to the sides. Zöe had taken a fresh towel, which she put, still folded, in her lap.

Zöe said, seriously, "Sam, a lot of people in The Netherlands use spanking as a sexual turn-on. There are even spanking clubs."

I nodded, "I know – although, as I said, I've never actually been to one of those clubs." I chuckled and, looking at Sarah next to me, said, "Now, if Sarah would come with me ..." She just shook her head, as I had expected.

I continued the story. "Along came the Internet. What an education I got! Over several years, I learned about many sexual persuasions, kinks, fantasies, and fetishes. I first read the newsgroups. Then, I looked at the images. And finally, we got full videos of incredible scenes. I watched bare bottom spankings, paddlings, tawsings, birchings, canings, and whippings. I learned about sadism and masochism, bondage and discipline ... and medical sex. It was enthralling and freeing to see the range of sexual fantasy, and realize that 'Hey, *I'm* relatively normal!'"

Henk raised his head from the chaise, "Medical sex?"

I swallowed hard, "That's the second turn-on. Things like giving shots. And enemas." I glanced at Sarah; she had a neutral face. Of course, she knew all of this, and I had expected her to stop me long before all this had come out. Although it hadn't been her job to 'stop me'; and I hadn't stopped myself.

"As a kid, I hated going to the doctor's office, and especially dreaded getting shots. In those days, they seemed to have bigger needles, jabbed them in without caring about your pain, and always tricked you into getting ready for it (at least that was my experience). I always fought, and would often have to be held down. It was unbelievable to me that anyone would let someone do this to them. My sisters had their tonsils out, and had to get penicillin shots several times per day. They told me about this, and I was fascinated by their individual reactions.

"Just before we were married, Sarah had a very bad flu – and we were planning to travel to France on our honeymoon. I went with her to the doctor, and watched while she was examined. Her doctor eventually proclaimed, 'Well, all you need is some penicillin, today and tomorrow, and then we'll see how you're doing.' My mouth dropped open – Sarah didn't put up any argument, but said, 'OK', and she went to the nurse's station to request her shot. They directed her to a small room; I went in with her, and she told me to sit on the chair.

"Rather quickly, the nurse came in with a tray, and closed the door. Without being told, Sarah pulled up her skirt, lowered her pantyhose and panties, and got onto the table face down. Before she was even settled, the nurse picked up a huge syringe, and plunged the needle into her bottom. Sarah didn't make a peep, but the nurse asked her about our upcoming wedding, and Sarah talked with her calmly, while she was being injected! It was a surreal, and very exciting experience for me – to see the compliance, acceptance, and trust required to bare yourself, put yourself in position, and then hold that position, while you are receiving pain."

Sarah objected, "First of all, you know it isn't much pain ..."

I broke in, "I know that *now*."

Sarah continued, "and I was really sick. My sickness was much more 'painful' than a couple of shots that would take less than a minute." She looked at Henk and Zöe, "He's such a baby!" They smiled, and waited for me to continue.

"As you know, I became a pharmaceutical researcher, and learned a lot about medicine. I had access to syringes and needles, and did some experiments on myself; for example, to understand what different size needles felt like. And I even learned how to give myself intramuscular injections. So I finally got over my fear of needles and shots."

I smiled, "Sarah, of course, has always been unafraid of getting shots. So she allowed me to practice inserting 1.5" needles into her hip. And she inserted a few needles in my butt. I found that she was right: Needle insertions don't actually hurt much – especially with a small gauge needle. But it is psychologically painful for many people, and I still get turned-on watching someone pull down their pants, bend over, and have a needle inserted into their bottom, as you talk with them.

"And, from seeing images and watching videos on certain websites, I realized that my fixation – or fetish – focuses on a woman's bottom: Both the spankings and the shots. And things like taking a rectal temperature, or administering an enema.

"I'm not a good enough psychologist to tell you exactly *why* all these experiences became a turn-on for me. But as I have fantasized about them, they have grown and combined into a 'fetish', or 'kink' – I guess you would say – for female submission to receiving a physical or psychological 'pain in the butt'."

Henk was lying on the chaise, his robe barely on his shoulders and open everywhere else, his eyes closed. "So you're a 'butt man'." He chuckled. "What's so unusual about that?" Henk then opened his eyes, and looked at me. "It doesn't mean that I would be turned-on by those things, but I can certainly understand them." I thought that this was a perfect example of Dutch tolerance.

Zöe said, "I don't think it's so strange. Then she looked into my eyes and smiled, "But I'm not going to let you spank me or stick needles in me!" She laughed. Then she looked at Henk, and back to me, stopped her laughing, and said, "Sam, do you know what 'needle play' is?"

I was astounded. "Yeah, sure. I've seen it on the Internet. I've even stuck a needle through a pinch of my own skin to see how it would feel. I found that it hurts a lot more coming out than going in."

Zöe laughed, and said, "That's right. One of my girlfriends is into that, as an art form. She's done a lot of extreme things. I'll give you her website to look at. I said I wouldn't let *you* do it ... but I let her try needle play on me, once." I'm sure my mouth was hanging open, my eyes as wide as my mouth. Zöe continued, "I didn't like it much.

There's an endorphin rush, but I'm really not into the pain of being skewered by a few dozen needles."

I said, sheepishly, "I guess you guys aren't just tolerant ... but have experienced a few of these kinds of things ... from the fetish world."

Zöe nodded and, under her breath, I heard a whispered 'You have no idea'.

We went into the sauna one last time, and I flipped the wooden holder for the hourglass, and watched the sand filter through the narrow waist of the glass tube. The time was marked on the wood, in one-minute increments from 1 to 15. I usually couldn't make it past twelve minutes.

We all took our places on the sauna benches, and I poured another ladle of water on the hot coals. Ten minutes passed without a word said by anyone; we heard only the slight hissing of the rocks. We all looked at each other and nodded, then silently filed out of the sauna and into the shower. This time, we would need to soap up. I looked at Zöe and asked, "May I bathe you?"

Zöe smiled sweetly at me and said, "Thanks for the offer. No." She then turned to Sarah, and asked, "Sarah, would *you* please bathe me?" We all laughed. Sarah just shrugged, and took the bar of soap, as I adjusted the temperature. The girls bathed each other – it looked like fun – while Henk and I bathed ourselves. I looked up at Henk, and frowned, "Sorry, Henk. I'm a little homophobic" (which I meant as 'I'm not comfortable being touched by men', although as I later found out, it means not accepting of gay people). He smiled, and as he continued washing, I'm sure I heard him say 'Me, too'. Then, he was chuckling, and I wondered if there was some inside joke.

After our shower, we all went upstairs to dress for dinner. Sarah and I scrambled downstairs to get all of the dishes started; they were prepped, and we just had to throw the ingredients together, and start cooking. I opened a nice bottle of wine, took out the crystal glasses, and set the table. The dinner came out great – perhaps not up to the standards of Amsterdam or Utrecht, but everyone devoured it.

The evening was nice – we talked about things ranging from geopolitics to the latest movies. We had left the subject of sex behind, and had an uneventful night.

The next morning, after breakfast, Henk and Zöe prepared to depart on the rest of their U.S. tour. Henk invited us to visit again, and promised he would take me to an interesting club. Zöe seconded the visit suggestion, and said she would take Sarah to a different interesting club. They also said it was their turn to take us to one of the local Dutch saunas. We said our goodbyes, and told them we looked forward to coming to The Netherlands again. For a visit. And perhaps some new experiences.

CHAPTER 3: SHEILA'S PARTY

One night, a few months after Henk and Zöe's visit, while Sarah was on a business trip, I went to a party in the neighborhood. The hosts – and a few of the guests – were getting high and a bit drunk. The wife, Sheila, was showing off - trying to ride her son's new skateboard - when she fell on the driveway, and thought she had broken her arm. We took her inside, and iced the arm; it didn't seem to be broken, but she was in some pain.

She will use any excuse to get drugs, so she asked me if my wife might have any pills that she could take, to ease the pain. This formed the germ of an idea. Sheila is quite suggestible, and I knew that the "placebo effect" might actually make her feel better. I began to develop a new fantasy, as I considered what I would do.

I left the party, walked home quickly, and grabbed some supplies, putting them into a small shaving bag. I carried it back to the party, and found Sheila in her room, with a girlfriend visiting from the East Coast. She looked up at me with hope, and asked, "Did your wife have anything?"

I told her, "No – but I have something that might help. You do realize that I'm not a medical doctor?"

"Yeah, but I know you know a lot about medicine."

"Well, I can give you a shot that might help. But it's a big shot, and has to be given intramuscularly."

She said, without emotion, "You mean in the butt? That's OK, I don't mind, if you think it will help."

I was amazed. Now, I went for the next phase of my fantasy. "I can't promise anything, but everything is sterile and safe, and it might be worth a try. However, I do have one 'condition' for giving you the shot ... you know I am a scientist, and love to do experiments ..." I tried to keep a straight face.

Continuing in my 'research scientist' mode, I explained, "When you fell, there was obviously inflammation. That will cause more metabolic activity (to carry away damaged cells, and build new cells – which become scar tissue), and that raises the temperature locally. If it's bad enough, it might raise your core body temperature very slightly. If we had just been able to measure it before the accident ..."

She was listening, but seemed overwhelmed by my detail. "Anyway, my idea is to measure your temperature very accurately now, then give you the shot, and measure again in 30-45 minutes – and see if the shot might have brought your temperature down. It may be a wild idea, but an interesting experiment. To get an accurate temperature, I borrowed my wife's basal metabolic thermometer – she used it to time her cycles a long time ago. Your temperature has to be taken rectally."

Sheila reacted, but calmed immediately. "Oh! Well, I guess I could let you do that."

This was confirmation of how out-of-it she really was ... but she was like this at every party. Her friend started to feel uncomfortable, having been shocked by hearing this exchange, so let herself out of the room, closing the door quietly.

I looked at Sheila, and said, "Then, let's get your temperature started. Just lower your pants at least down to mid-thigh, and lie on the bed."

She unfastened her belt, and unzipped her blue jeans, pushing them down; they fell nearly down to her ankles. She turned toward the bed, lowering her underwear and lying face down on the bed. She pulled the pillow to her, and watched, as I took out a small tube of KY and lubricated the thermometer. I sat down on the edge of the bed next to her, and separated her buttocks. She chuckled.

I asked, "Are you ready?" She just nodded.

As the thermometer touched her anus and she felt the cold KY, she flinched a little; I had anticipated this, and held the thermometer there until she had settled-down. I then pushed the thermometer smoothly into her, until only about an inch was protruding from her anus.

She moaned a little, but didn't show any other reaction. I moved the thermometer back and forth, around in circles, and slowly in and out of her, while eruditely explaining, "We need to have perfect thermal conductivity between your rectal mucosa and the thermometer."

After 15-20 seconds of watching the thermometer move in and out of her, I left an inch sticking out, and let go of her buttocks. I told her, "Please lie very still, and keep quiet, so we can get an accurate temperature." Sheila closed her eyes, and I started the timer on my watch for four minutes.

I then went into the bathroom and washed my hands, came back to the bedroom, placing the shaving bag on the nightstand, and unloaded the contents. I opened the sterile packages, and assembled the syringe and needle. I then took out a vial of sterile saline for injection, and cleaned the top with an alcohol swab. I drew 5 cc of air into the syringe, and stuck the needle through the latex barrier in the top of the vial. I injected the air into the vial, and then turned the vial and syringe over, and drew out 5 cc of sterile saline. I made sure there were no bubbles, and tested the stream by injecting a small amount into the air.

I asked Sheila, "Are you ready for your shot now?"

She replied, "Sure."

I sat next to her again on the edge of the bed, and asked her, "Right side OK? If you want another one in 45 minutes, we can do it on the other side."

She said, "That's OK." I located the injection site in the upper outer quadrant of her right buttock, swabbed it with alcohol, and uncapped the needle. With my left hand, I held her tissue taught, and told her, "Take a couple of deep breaths, and try to relax your bottom."

I positioned the needle above her skin, and said, "Here we go ..." then quickly plunged the needle into her flesh. I pulled back a bit on the plunger of the syringe to make sure I wasn't in a blood vessel. Sheila seemed quite calm, so I asked her, "How are you doing?"

She replied, "Fine ... so far."

I proceeded to inject her slowly, taking 30-40 seconds to empty the syringe. "You still OK?"

She was unfazed, "I'm OK. Is it almost done?"

I unwrapped a 2x2 gauze pad, placed it next to the needle, withdrew the needle quickly and, putting some pressure on the gauze, told her, "You're done."

She said, "That wasn't too bad."

I reminded her, "Now lay still and quiet, so we can finish your temperature." I placed a small round Band-Aid over the injection site.

I disassembled the syringe and needle, putting them into a baggie for disposal when I got back home, and put everything back into the shaving bag. I sat down next to Sheila, separated her buttocks, and began slowly moving the thermometer in and out a couple of inches. "Does that feel OK?"

She answered, "I guess."

About that time, my watch timer buzzed, and I removed the thermometer. I used a tissue to clean it, and read the temperature. "99.85 degrees Fahrenheit – that seems reasonable. We'll have to see what happens in 45 minutes."

I told Sheila that she could get up, as I stepped into the bathroom to wash the thermometer. A minute later – appearing rested – she casually stood up facing me and pulled up her underwear, but stepped out of her pants. Carrying them, she walked past me into the bathroom, and sat on the toilet to pee. I quickly finished and went back into the bedroom to pack up the thermometer.

Sheila came out of the bathroom, zipping up her blue jeans, and straightening her top. She said, "Thank you!"

I replied, "Let's see if you feel better, and we'll take your temperature again in a while. If you think the shot helped, you can ask me to give you another one." She just smiled at me, turned and opened the door, and went back into the party.

Of course, we went back into the bedroom and repeated nearly the same thing, taking Sheila's temperature, and even giving her a second shot. I thought she was turned-on by the experience, although I never said or did anything remotely sexual while I was with her. This experience further fueled my interest in spanking, medical sex, and submission. And, I realized that I could get nearly as turned-on by openness, as by submission.

CHAPTER 4: THE ACCIDENT

About a year after Henk and Zöe's visit, we still had not visited them in Holland. My wife had to make a business trip to London and Sheffield, and I suggested that I join her, and we would take Henk and Zöe up on their offer. But Sarah's agenda was packed, and she had meetings scheduled in New York immediately after her London meetings. We decided that we would plan a trip later in the year, and I e-mailed Henk, giving him a heads-up, and asking the best dates for us to visit.

I was at home, on the computer, planning our next trip – it would be one of the first 'vacation' trips we had taken in quite a while – when I got the call. Sarah had been driving around a traffic circle, when another driver plowed into her. My wife had been driving on the correct side of the road, but the other driver – another American – hadn't, and my love left my life as quickly as she had entered it twenty five years before. I was devastated, crushed. My sons, now living on each side of the country, came back home, and we cried together. Sarah and I had been with each other for half of our lives, and I couldn't imagine my life going on without her.

Now alone in a large house, I grieved for more than two years. Many of my friends, including close female friends, tried to console me, and made introductions to very nice women. But I was not interested in developing another relationship. I considered selling the house, but I was too depressed, too lethargic, and too numb to take any action.

I spent an increasing amount of time looking at images and videos on the Internet – yes, you might say 'porn', but it was very educational, even for someone as liberal, experienced and sexually creative as I thought I had been. It was a diversion, an escape: Into fantasies of pain, from the reality of pain – *real* pain.

I learned much more about domination and submission, the roles of the 'top' (spanker) and 'bottom' (spankee), the 'dom' (male dominant) and 'domme' (female dominant; if done professionally, usually called a dominatrix), how to use various implements, how to create tension and suspense in the spanking partner, and how – as a top – to keep everything safe.

I watched videos of spanking role play, of medical sex – including gynecologic exams, shots, enemas – and many other fetishes ... most of which I could not relate to, but nearly all of which were surprising, in terms of how many people seemed to be involved in these activities.

I frequented Internet stores that specialized in spanking, D&S, and B&D, and began making regular purchases of punishment implements, accessories and supplies. The implements included paddles, whips, tawses, floggers, hairbrushes, wooden spoons, belts, and canes of various sizes and shapes. Some of these were meant for intense experiences, while others were fairly mild. I tried most of these on myself, but there was no way to spank myself realistically.

I purchased gloves that enabled stroking someone with soft fur. I bought bespoke accessories, such as soft padded wrist and ankle straps with metal hooks, and blindfolds. And I bought acupuncture needles, and a large stock of medical supplies, including syringes and needles, sterile saline, alcohol swabs and gauze pads, and even a few instruments – a lighted speculum, anoscope, and a stirrup set-up that clamped onto a desk.

I spent nearly a year building out the basement, and decorating – with Berber carpeting, a nice couch and loveseat, coffee table, comfortable chair, and wet bar at one end of the room, and a king size bed at the other end that was made private by a curtain that closed off the other end of the room. I mounted a very large motorized projection screen in the ceiling behind the curtain; it was nearly the width of the room, and came down to the floor. I modified a modern, platform bed, mounting center speakers at the base of the platform, and covering it with fabric that matched the furniture. I also acquired, at a second-hand store, an old-fashioned armless 'spanking' chair and a couple of small stools.

Thus, the 'playroom' could be used as a theater, lowering the screen, and opening the motorized curtains, with no hint that a bed lurked behind. I also installed small spotlights in various strategic locations on the ceiling, which I could turn on or off, and dim, using a handheld computerized remote control, as well as video equipment to record everything that happened in my 'playroom'. I don't call it a 'dungeon', and do not have heavy bondage equipment, as might be expected by some aficionados. Instead, I made the room into a softly lit, romantic cave-like environment.

Also downstairs was a small bedroom, across from the sauna, that we had used as a storage room. I kept some of the casual clothes I wore day-to-day in that room, and often came down, after waking, for a sauna and shower, before getting dressed for the day.

I had some ideas for the spare bedroom. As I already had a nice big bed in the playroom, I considered putting a cot and chest of drawers into the room that I now imagined as Spartan 'quarters' for a sex slave. But I never developed these fantasies or the room, so kept it locked and mostly forgotten.

At the end of the year, I retired, as planned; I no longer had the motivation to do any serious work, and looked forward to taking it easy ... and maybe enjoying some of my fantasies with a partner. But I had no idea how I would find a willing – even enthusiastic – play partner, especially one who would engage in role-play, and share some of my fetishistic interests.

CHAPTER 5: NEIGHBORLY NEIGHBOR

After nearly three years without Sarah, I was lonely and craving companionship; but I didn't think I would ever be ready for 'dating' again – I had no desire to re-marry, or develop a long-term relationship.

As I was retired, and home most days, I became friendly with my next-door neighbor, Liz, whose husband was an oil executive, and often away on international business travel. Liz had been a massage therapist, and had worked as a beautician. She introduced me to the other women in the shop and explained some of the procedures in which they specialized, which seemed well suited to a masochistic client.

In the spring, Liz and I started playing tennis a couple of mornings a week, and we rode our bikes through a local wooded area, on dirt paths that bounced us around until we were laughing hysterically.

We had fun on our outings, and grew closer together emotionally. Liz shared with me the trials and tribulations of marriage to her demanding and dictatorial husband. They had grown apart, and she had great resentment about being told what to do all the time; so she had begun developing a life of her own.

Liz and I were comfortable with our friendship, and we both knew it would become nothing more than companionship, and having some fun experiences together.

One early summer day, Liz suggested that we ride our bikes farther – to a beautiful stream she had found when she first moved into the area. We rode along a dirt path to the stream, with sunlight filtering through the trees, and dappling her lithe body on the bike ahead of me, in stop-motion, as with a strobe light.

Liz was a beautiful woman, with small breasts, but a curvaceous body. She always seemed to have a smile (except when talking about her husband), and was what I considered a "fun-loving" person. I couldn't help but notice Liz' hips falling over the tiny bike seat, as they moved up and down hypnotically. I nearly fell off my bike when my front tire hit a large stone I had not noticed, my eyes being glued on Liz' lovely bottom. Her blond hair shined with shimmers of light that were constantly moving – again, it seemed, hypnotically.

She stopped her bike when we reached the stream, and leaned it against a nearby tree. Liz looked up at me, smiling mischievously, and said, "Come on, this way!" She brightly walked across a log to the other side of the stream where, I now saw, another path led off into the forest.

I followed her, admiring the beautiful surroundings, the perfect weather, and her rear end – in tight shorts – swaying rhythmically as we walked down the trail. We suddenly came into a clearing, where the stream widened into a broad pool, with several large flat-topped boulders, and a huge overhanging willow tree, making this an enchanting setting.

As I walked into the clearing, Liz was already at the water's edge. She looked back at me with a very sensual smile, then turned back towards the pond and removed her blouse; she wasn't wearing a bra. As I approached her, I said, "What are you doing?" She turned towards me, as she tugged down her pants and underwear, and said "I'm going in the water, silly!"

With that, she took a first step into the water, and let her body fall forward, almost surreally, into the pond as I looked on – with my eyes widening and my jaw dropping. I have always been open about nudity, but I had no idea that Liz was. I quickly removed my clothes, and joined her in the cool, clear water.

We had a great morning playing in the water, and lying in the sun afterward, starting an 'all-over tan' for the summer. We talked about many things, mainly our hopes and desires, places we would like to travel, and things we would like to do. I still have a long 'bucket-list' that encompasses travel, sports, hobbies … and living some of the fantasies that I had, for so long, developed. I didn't know whether I would actually do any of these things, without being able to share them with Sarah.

I told Liz how important sex had been in my life, and that I still have many fantasies … but now have to "take care of myself" when I get horny. She sighed, and told me that her sex life with her husband was sporadic, and that he never tended to her sexual needs. I asked her, "So, do you masturbate?"

She looked away, into the forest, and finally said, "Yes, of course." She was starting to blush – a bit strange, as she was totally nude, and comfortable with that, but not with our conversation.

I looked at her, and finally worked up the nerve to ask, "What positions do you use to masturbate?"

She again hesitated, but then said quietly, "Usually lying on my stomach, or sometimes sitting back in a chair."

We were quiet for what seemed like several minutes, but it was probably only 15-20 seconds. I then asked, "Would you share some of your fantasies with me?"

Liz looked at me, and replied, "I'm not really that comfortable telling you this stuff – it's pretty private. What are YOUR fantasies?"

That was my opening. I am mature enough to know that opportunities like this do not happen often. I did not want to scare off my neighbor, but it seemed like we were close enough to be able to share these things. I did not tell her about my playroom, but I did begin to explain to her how I am turned on by things like women submitting to a spanking.

She wasn't sure what to make of that, just nodded and said, "OK."

I told her that she would understand better what I was talking about, if she would let me show her some images and videos on certain websites.

She again said, "OK." She had a distant look, and I really had no idea whether my revelation had turned her on or off. I hoped I hadn't just lost her friendship.

A little later, Liz told me that she had to be getting back home, as she was expecting a delivery that afternoon and had to sign for it. We rode our bikes back, and she offered me some refreshment in her kitchen.

As she returned from the refrigerator with a pitcher of lemonade, she suddenly set it down on the counter, turned to me, and gave me a big hug. "Thank you for being a friend," she said. We then drank our lemonade, lost in our own thoughts.

Liz finally got up, and said, "Well, I've got to get showered, before the Fed Ex guy gets here."

I half-jokingly said, "Great! I'd *love* to take a shower with you!"

She laughed, and then stopped, looked at me, and asked, "Are you serious?"

That stunned me, but I recovered quickly, and said, "Sure, if you're up for some good clean fun! We've been nude together all morning, so what's the big deal?"

She looked down at the ground for a full minute, and I started getting worried that I had pushed things too far; I really didn't want to jeopardize our friendship. I told her, "Sorry – I didn't mean to get you upset. I was just joking ... kind-of. Actually, it really would be fun to bathe each other. JUST bathe ... if you wouldn't take it the wrong way."

She looked up at me and said, "You're a really nice guy, and I do trust you. But I'm very dedicated to my husband ... as difficult as he is, sometimes."

I told her, "Well, I was dedicated to my wife for more than two decades, but we accepted openness with our friends. She wouldn't think anything of me taking a shower with one of my female friends, or even spending a night in the same bed ... provided we didn't have sex. Of course, I always told my wife about the things I did with my friends: I never tried to hide anything."

She said, "I understand that, but my husband wouldn't – so I couldn't possibly tell him about our friendship; even what we did today would get him upset ... and nothing happened!"

We looked at each other for a moment, and I said, "Again, I'm sorry. I don't want to get you in trouble with your husband."

That was the turning point. Liz considered herself independent and couldn't stand the thought that her husband would prohibit her from doing things she liked. Liz looked at me, and quietly said, "Come on, let's go upstairs."

She unbuttoned her blouse as we climbed the stairs, and we went into the master bedroom, where we undressed together without saying a word. I put my clothes on the bed, and we went into the bathroom.

She said, "I have to pee, but you can get in the shower and get started."

So I stepped into the large, tiled double shower, which was open to the room. I turned on and adjusted the water, and stepped under the stream, facing away from Liz, who was sitting on the toilet. I squeezed some of her shampoo from the bottle, and started washing my hair – with my eyes closed to prevent soap from getting in them.

A moment later, I felt Liz bump against me, as she entered the shower. I heard a faucet being turned, and a second showerhead sprung to life. When I opened my eyes, Liz was washing her shoulder-length, blond hair, and smiling at me, her lips moist, and her teeth sparkling. It was one of the most beautiful smiles I have ever seen!

When we finished shampooing, I turned Liz around to face the stream of warm water on her side of the shower. I began soaping her back, her neck, her arms, and her underarms. I put the bar of soap down, and massaged all of these areas with my hands. I then took the soap and worked my way down … to her beautiful bottom.

Liz seemed quite content to let me bathe her. I spent some time squeezing and molding her twin globes in my hands, as I worked the soap into the crack between her buttocks, and smoothly slipped my hand down so that my fingers were at her anus.

I washed her with my fingers curving around her perineum and, as Liz still had not made a sound, slipped a finger deeply into her rectum. I heard Liz' sharp intake of breath, but she remained still. I moved my finger around, and then in and out – all taking probably less than 5 seconds, but it had to be one of the most intimate things I had done with a woman other than my wife, since I had gotten married.

I knelt down, and continued bathing Liz, working my way down the backs of her legs, and washing her feet, as Liz put her hand on my shoulder to steady herself, and lifted each foot, in turn, off the shower tile. I took the hand-held shower attachment, and hosed her backside down, from neck to feet, and then asked Liz to turn around.

I kneeled, with my head at her crotch-level, as I worked my way up her legs to her thighs. I washed each of her upper thighs with one of my hands between her legs, but only grazing her pubic hair.

I stood up, and asked, "How are you doing?"

She quickly replied, "I'm fine. You're doing a great job bathing me!"

I then took the bar of soap, and moved it over her pubic hair to create a lot of lather, and slid my other hand down, using my middle finger to slightly part her labia on each down-stroke, and slipped my finger inside her, moving it around, and then quickly back out, and continued washing her hips and waist.

Liz moaned, and whispered, "The soap burns down there!" I used the hand-held showerhead to rinse her pubic hair area, and took the opportunity to once again let my hand slip down, and put a finger into her to get some water in, and the soap out. Liz didn't say anything but seemed amused by my actions.

I continued soaping her body, moving up across her stomach, and over and around her small breasts. I spent some time washing her breasts, squeezing them, and running my fingers lightly over, and then pinching her nipples, which seemed to instantly become erect. I heard a moan, and saw that Liz' eyes were closed.

I turned her around, facing the shower again, and rinsed her off – doing another once-over with my hands across her body. I stood behind her, pressing my front to her back, reaching my arms around to hold her breasts.

Then I turned her around, and gave her a big hug, and said "Thank you. I hope you enjoyed that as much as I did."

Liz looked up at me, bit her lip, and said in a low, serious voice, "That was really nice." She hugged me, then said, brightly, "Now, it's my turn!"

I stepped back from her, ready to turn around to face the showerhead on my side. She glanced down, and then exclaimed, "I'm really surprised that you don't have an erection! Aren't I a turn-on for you?"

I stepped towards her, and held her shoulders firmly in my hands, looking directly into her eyes. "Yes Liz, you are a beautiful woman, and an incredible turn-on. If you weren't married, I'd be very tempted to ravage you right now. But our friendship is very important to me, and I don't want to spoil it by coming on to you."

Liz looked into my eyes – I imagined tears coming from hers, but it was undoubtedly just the shower water streaming down from her hair.

She said, "Our friendship is important to me, too. You know I wouldn't have even thought of doing something like this with anyone else ... but I trust you, and know you wouldn't do anything I didn't want. And I trust myself. Sorry, if this disappoints you, but I'm not planning on having sex with you, or anyone besides my husband."

I said sincerely, "Liz, it's not a disappointment. It wasn't expected. And, I'd rather we remain as long-term friends than as short-term lovers."

Liz nodded, and said, "Thank you. But I would still like to know how you can have such self-control, with us both nude in the shower, and you bathing my private parts."

I replied, "Well, you know I've gone to nude beaches for many years, so I don't automatically get turned-on every time I see a nude woman, even a beautiful woman like you, at close range. I've taken showers with other women, on a friendly basis. I could certainly get turned-on within a minute or two, if I started fantasizing, or thinking about us making love, or if I started 'doing' myself ... but I won't do that. Unless, you really want to see what I look like with an erection?"

Liz chuckled, and said, "No, that's OK. I prefer you this way. But don't worry if it happens; I don't feel threatened by you."

I turned to face the shower stream, and Liz bathed me, slowly – showing off her expertise at massage. It felt wonderful.

She worked her way down my back, and roughly grabbed and squeezed my buttocks. She put the bar of soap at the top of my butt crack, and began sliding it back and forth, lower and lower, until it was over my anus. I felt her hand sliding down, and was stunned when she slipped a finger into me. She pushed it in further, and bent the tip of her finger so that it was pressing against my prostate. I must have moaned involuntarily, as she laughed, and said, "Yes, I'm familiar with anatomy, too. I thought you might like this."

My breathing became heavier, and I felt a stirring that I could not avoid. Liz must have realized this, as she reached around, and took my penis in her hand, squeezing gently, and then stroking it, in time with the movement of her finger that was still in my rectum, rhythmically pressing on my prostate.

We were silent, and I only wished that this would go on forever. I did start to get hard, and Liz laughed again, and said, "See, I knew you weren't that strong! I guess now that I've got you going, we'll just have to finish, so you're relaxed again." She kept up the movement with both of her hands, while she pressed her breasts up against my back.

By this time, my breathing was ragged, and I knew I wasn't far from having an orgasm. Liz whispered, "It's OK. It's the least I can do for you, after you've been so nice to me. You really are a gentleman. And now, you'll be rewarded."

I couldn't say anything – hardly think anything – as Liz circled her fingers around my erection, and moved her hand up and down my length, squeezing exactly at the right time.

It didn't take long, and I came violently, my body shaking, and my breath catching. I realized that this was the first orgasm I had had with someone since my wife had died. I spurted and spurted, and then began sobbing. Liz turned me around, and pressed up against me, hugging me tightly.

CHAPTER 6: TOPPING LIZ

Liz and I rode to the pond often throughout the summer. We did not talk about our shower experience, but had become entirely open with each other, both physically, and psychologically. If we were in the forest and Liz needed to pee, she would step off the trail a few feet, squat and pee – just pulling the crotch of her shorts and underwear aside.

When I went next door to get Liz for a bike ride, or tennis game, she would bring me upstairs, where I stood in the bedroom doorway, and watched her get changed while we talked. On one of these occasions, she mentioned that I still hadn't shown her those spanking websites we had talked about. I had not forgotten about this, but hadn't wanted to push too hard and possibly spoil our good relationship.

After she finished changing into her tennis outfit, we went into the den, and sat down in front of her computer. I fired up the browser, and typed in a URL. The webpage flashed onto the screen, with dozens of small thumbnails, showing girls getting spanked, their red bottoms on display.

Liz gasped, and her eyes widened. I clicked on a thumbnail, and a video began playing. I switched to full-screen and turned up the volume.

Liz and I watched, as a girl entered the headmaster's office, was lectured-to, and then punished with an over-the-knee spanking and a strapping. The girl shrieked, and her bright red bottom quivered, but she held herself in place while the headmaster thrashed her. Liz stiffened as she watched each stroke of the heavy strap land on the girl's bottom.

We watched several more videos – husbands spanking wives, teachers spanking students, boyfriends spanking girlfriends, and a few girl-on-girl spankings, as well. They all looked very real: It was clear that these girls really were taking a hard spanking. Not in the role they were playing, but as young actresses, willing to do the video (and take the spanking) for hard cash. In any case, they were really feeling pain, and they really were holding themselves in place voluntarily.

As usual, I became incredibly turned-on watching these videos. Although Liz had gasped and flinched initially, she became quiet as she stared at the screen, watching the girls taking their spankings. I saw her hand settle between her legs, her fingers moving very slightly; her face was definitely flushed – nearly as red as the bottoms on her computer monitor.

As one of the videos ended, she suddenly looked over at me, quickly pulled her hand from between her legs, and opened her mouth to say something, but then closed her mouth and quickly looked away, and then back at me. Her face reddened even more.

She exclaimed, "You're right! This stuff is pretty hot. I wouldn't have believed it, but I can understand – at least a little bit – why it turns you on."

I sat with my hands in my lap, trying (probably unsuccessfully) to hide the erection that was pressing upward on my pants. Liz turned off the computer, and reached across the desk for a small pad of pink notepaper, took a sheet and a pen, and started writing. She said that we should get going to our tennis game, but that she had something for me when we got back.

Our tennis game was ridiculous – I don't think either one of us could concentrate for more than two seconds. We gave up early, and drove back home. As we walked up her front steps, she said, "Wait a minute, I have to get something."

I was a bit put-off that she didn't invite me in (as my mind drifted to the shower we had taken together). I couldn't imagine what she was getting, or why I had to stand outside.

Liz returned to the door, and told me that she would have to start cooking dinner, as her husband was due to return that evening. She thanked me for the tennis game, and for sharing the websites with her. She had a small grin (or grimace?) that I could not interpret. She then hugged me, and gave me the small pink note, folded in half. "Thanks again for the day. I'll see you later."

All I could say was, "Bye," as Liz closed the front door in my face.

I walked to my house, and went down to the playroom. I was thinking about Liz and I watching the spanking videos together, and I began to get turned on again. I took a beer from the fridge in the bar, and plopped down on the couch. As I took a first swallow of beer, I looked down at the pink note and unfolded it. It read:

Subject:	Punishment for misbehavior
Reason:	Not satisfying husband's needs
Punishment:	As deserved
When:	August 11, 1PM

I choked, and the beer came spraying out of my mouth, all over the new coffee table. Liz had just seen the videos, and she evidently had written this note without even thinking about it. Or, perhaps she had been thinking about it since I first mentioned my spanking fantasies at the pond that first time we were there in the spring? This was too good to be true!

Then, I started thinking about it (OK, I never STOPPED thinking about it!). What, exactly, would we do? I didn't want to really hurt her, but she had seen the girls cry and their bottoms turn red with welts ... and she still had voluntarily asked for me to punish her! And what did she mean by "as deserved"? Was she leaving the punishment up to me?

August 11 was only a week away, and now that I finally had the opportunity to live one of my fantasies, I wasn't sure what I wanted to do, specifically. Yes, I would bare her bottom. Yes, I would put her over my knee for an old-fashioned hand spanking. But, then what? Could I really cane her? Would she ever talk to me after that? Or, worse yet, would she charge me with assault? The more I thought about it, the more confused I became.

Slowly, over the next few days, the 'spanking plan' came together. I didn't know if the actual 'live event' would be a turn-on, but I must have masturbated at least six times per day, thinking about the plan, and fantasizing how it would go.

I prepared the playroom, and made sure the implements were in their places, and the video system was working. I hadn't decided whether I would video the session, but then I realized that the video would be proof that Liz wanted this experience, and that I wasn't forcing her. I re-arranged the lighting, and installed a couple more focused spotlights in key positions on the ceiling.

I made sure the bathroom was clean, and the spare bedroom (that I had now earmarked as my medical exam room) was locked. I thought about some medical scenarios, but really wasn't ready, yet, to share this part of my fantasy with Liz. Well, maybe I could introduce her to a few needles. I e-mailed Liz, suggesting that she wear full-size underwear, and a full, loose dress to her punishment session, and told her that I was looking forward to helping her correct her pattern of misbehavior.

I didn't receive an e-mail reply back from her, and hoped that Liz hadn't reconsidered. The week passed quickly, and finally the scheduled punishment day arrived. At precisely 1PM, I heard a knock on the front door. I opened it, and Liz came in. We hugged briefly, and I asked her to follow me downstairs to the basement.

She said, "I didn't know you had finished the basement!"

I told her, "Yes, after Sarah died, I've had lots of time for projects, so I built my 'man cave' down here."

I could tell that she was impressed with the finish of the room. I had the drape closed at the other end of the room, behind which the bed was located. There was nothing to indicate that the room was anything other than a den or study. In addition to the couch and coffee table, I had, in an "L" part of the room, a modern walnut and stainless steel desk with a large executive chair behind it, and two smaller swivel chairs with low backs and padded arms in front of it.

I asked Liz if she wanted something to drink, and she decided that a glass of wine might help calm her. She really did look nervous. I stepped behind the bar, and poured two glasses of Grgich chardonnay, and then we sat on the couch. We raised our glasses in a toast, and drank a swallow of wine silently.

Then I asked her, "Do you really want to do this?"

She immediately said, "Yes ... I think so." Her cheeks were flushed, and her breathing shallow.

I looked into her eyes, and said, "You know, this will be a real punishment. Your bottom is going to hurt."

"I know," she said, as she swallowed hard.

I said sternly, "Liz, you know that what turns me on is your submission and your obedience; if we do this, I expect you to do everything that I ask, including removing your clothes, and getting into position for your spanking. And I expect you to hold your position throughout the spanking. You will address me as "Sir", and you will remain as quiet as possible, unless I ask you something. Do you understand?"

Liz looked down, and said 'Yes, Sir' so quietly that I would not have heard her if the air conditioning had come on.

We finished our glasses of wine, and I stood up from the couch. "Then let's get started. Come over and sit on this chair in front of the desk, and I'll explain how you will be punished."

I walked around the desk and sat in the executive chair, while Liz sat in one of the facing chairs. She looked different – smaller, more nervous, less self-confident; and her face was very flushed. I let her sit for several minutes, while I shuffled some papers.

I had actually written out a script for the punishment, as I didn't want to get flustered during my big opportunity. Liz was looking down at the hands she was wringing in her lap, and seemed nearly ready to cry. I wasn't sure what she was feeling, but there was a lot of emotion involved, and she was taking this very seriously – which was just what I wanted.

"Liz, I understand that you have been misbehaving?"

"Yes, Sir."

I asked, "What is the nature of your transgressions?"

Liz looked up and said, "I haven't been nice to my husband. I've been purposely forgetting to do things he asks, not making dinner for him some nights, and withholding sex – telling him that I'm not feeling well."

I said, "OK. Go on."

Liz looked down again, and quietly said, "I'm not sure if I love him or hate him. Right now, the last thing I feel like doing is making him happy. I know this is wrong – I'm his wife; I shouldn't be acting this way, but that's how I feel."

She continued, "I think a punishment might help me to improve." I couldn't tell whether this was role-play, or if she was serious.

I said, confidently, "Well, you've come to the right place. As you know, I run a spanking service – mainly to help couples wanting to reconcile after one of them has made some transgression. Usually, the husband comes to me, and requests that I punish his wife, who must agree to the punishment in writing. In this case, you're requesting the punishment yourself. It is unusual, but I am impressed with your desire to improve, and will do my best to deliver a sound punishment that you will not soon forget."

Liz looked up at me, her eyes filling with tears.

"You don't really run a punishment service, do you?" she suddenly asked, with a sparkle in her eyes. Ha! Now, *she* wasn't sure what was real and what was fantasy!

"No, Liz, this is just part of the role-play."

Liz looked down, and started wringing her hands again.

I told her to stand up, and come around the desk to me. She did so, and when we were standing face-to-face, I told her to turn around and put her hands on her head. She obeyed immediately and silently.

I then lifted the hem on the back of her dress, bringing it up all the way up to her shoulders. As instructed, Liz had worn full-size, plain white underwear. I reached over and grabbed a couple of small binder clips from my desk, and clipped the hem of her dress to the shoulder of the dress on each side. The dress, in back, was up above her waist, but from the front, it looked normal. I told her to go sit down in the chair.

"Liz, I have decided to administer a 'level-50' punishment today. I will explain what that means in a few minutes. First, you need to know that your punishment will consist of three parts: the main punishment, the corner-time, and any corrective punishment required."

Liz' mouth dropped open, and her eyes showed curiosity, but she remained silent.

I continued, "Your punishment will be given as five level-10 bare-bottom spankings, each using a different implement, and with you in a different position. When I tell you to get into a certain position, you will immediately do so, and remain in that position until told otherwise. Do you understand?"

"Yes, Sir."

I couldn't help but smile. "Good. You will also request each punishment, and thank me for each punishment afterward. Is that clear?"

"Yes, Sir."

I chuckled, realizing this had been the most times I had been addressed as 'Sir' in my entire life!

I continued lecturing her with the instructions. "You will not say a word, unless I ask you a question, and you must remain as quiet as possible. You MUST NOT reach back to shield your bottom or rub your bottom! This is very important. I don't want to swing a wooden paddle, and break all of your fingers because you suddenly reached back." Liz suddenly looked even more worried.

Notwithstanding Liz' look, I explained, "If you get out of position – for example, by moving your hands or feet, or standing up – you *will* receive additional punishment. This may consist of additional strokes of the same implement, strokes with a different (more severe) implement, re-starting that level of punishment again from the beginning, or adding some punishment during your corner time. The corrective punishment will be whatever I decide, and you will cooperate fully. Do you understand and agree?"

"Yes, Sir."

She really did appear as though she would start crying at any moment.

"The corner time will be 5 minutes for each level-10 punishment. Traditionally, corner time is used to show off the result of the spanking (a red bottom), and make the punishee stand with nothing to think about except her misbehavior and how she was punished. In our case, I will put you into whatever position I decide, and you will then take a rectal insertion, which will last for the full 5 minutes."

Liz' eyes widened, and her mouth opened further, but she didn't say anything, just nodded slowly.

I told Liz to stand up in front of the desk, spread her feet to shoulder-width, and put her hands on top of her head. "I call this the 'standing' position. You will get into this position whenever I have not told you to take another position. Do you understand?"

Again, Liz answered, "Yes, Sir."

"Good, because you *will* receive corrective punishment, if you disobey. Finally," I said, "when I ask you something, you will answer honestly, and if I ask you to make a choice, you will make it quickly without complaining. Do you understand?"

"Yes, Sir." Liz appeared overwhelmed; perhaps I had developed too much tension?

"OK. Would you like to pee, before we begin your spanking?"

She smiled sheepishly, and said, "Yes, please."

I said, "OK – you may go to the bathroom now. Leave the door open a crack. When you're finished, please wash your hands, and then come back and we'll get started."

Liz walked out of the playroom, and into the next-door bathroom. Based on the light still coming out, I knew she hadn't closed the door at all. I quickly opened a desk drawer, and pulled out some supplies. I was already getting turned-on, and we hadn't even begun her punishment, yet!

Liz walked back into the playroom. Watching her approach the desk, it was impossible to tell that the back of her dress was above her waist, with her underwear and legs exposed.

She said, "OK, I guess I'm ready. What do you want me to do?"

I just looked at her. "You know what to do!"

She looked confused, "I do? I don't think so ..."

I stood up behind the desk and, in my severest tone, said, "Liz, you have agreed to cooperate, haven't you?"

She jumped. "Yes, sir, of course!"

"And I told you that you would need to obey my instructions, and get into any position that I told you?"

"Yes, sir." Her face was questioning, and now showing great concern.

"I have only taught you one thing, so far, and that was to get into the standing position whenever I hadn't asked you to be in another position."

Liz straightened, and a surprised "Oh!" came out of her mouth. She quickly got back into the standing position in front of the desk.

"Liz, I told you that I would give you corrective punishment, if you didn't follow instructions, didn't I? And you agreed, didn't you?"

A very quiet "Yes, Sir" came from her lips, and it again looked like she was about to cry.

I said sadly, "OK. I was hoping that you wouldn't require corrective punishment until after your main punishment had begun, but you've left me with no choice. Stand about a foot in front of the desk." Liz obeyed immediately.

"Now, widen your stance, bend at the waist, and put your forearms on the desk, palms down."

Liz bent over, and put her hands on the desk. "I said 'your forearms' – not your hands. I want you bent over with your butt in the air!"

"Yes sir," she said, as she got down on her forearms, and held her head up, looking at me.

I came around the desk behind her. "I don't want to spank you now, because you need a good warm-up first. So I'll have to introduce another type of corrective punishment that you will receive if you don't take your spankings cooperatively."

With that, I lowered her underwear to just below her bottom. She gasped, unsure of what to expect next. I then walked back around to my chair, and sat down. Liz was watching me closely, as I picked up a small sterile package and opened it. After taking off the safety cap, I held up the 25-gauge, 1½" long stainless steel hypodermic needle for her to see. Her eyes widened, and she involuntarily sputtered out a "No!" before she realized that she should have been silent.

I looked at her, and shook my head, "Well, you seem to want more corrective punishment, so instead of inserting one needle, I'll insert one on each side." Liz was squirming, as much as she could while remaining in position. This punishment was already going in a different direction than she had expected ... but exactly as I had hoped.

I re-capped the first needle, and opened a second package, taking the two needles and an alcohol swab with me, as I walked around the desk behind Liz again. She nervously watched me, as I came around her, and I told her, "You will keep your eyes straight ahead during your punishments, and not look back at me. Do you understand?"

"Yes, Sir." She looked ahead, at my empty executive chair.

"I am going to insert one needle on each side, and they will be left in until I think you have learned your lesson to obey me. Which side would you like me to do first?"

"I don't know. Neither."

"Well, Liz, you have just earned ANOTHER corrective punishment!"

She started to stand up, and said, "What?!?!?"

I put my hand on her back and, with light pressure, she got back down into position. "Yes. I told you that if you were given a choice, you had to choose – not say 'I don't know' or 'neither'. You needed to say 'left' or 'right'. I am going to ask you again, and I want a complete sentence from you, Liz. On which side do you want me to insert the first needle?"

"I would like you to insert the first needle on the right side, Sir."

"Very good! That's what I wanted to hear."

"You've earned additional corrective punishment, so I could stick you twice on each side, or insert two needles on each side ..."

Again, Liz sputtered, "Oh, no! ..."

I had to shake my head. "Liz, you are an intelligent person, but you are not learning. What am I going to do with you? We haven't even begun the punishment, yet!"

"I'm sorry, Sir. I'll try harder."

I sighed, "OK. I'll give you a break, and only insert one needle on each side ... but the second insertion will be a slow one – those hurt more. And, I'll leave the needles in longer." I then swabbed the upper outer quadrant of her right buttock with alcohol – probably much higher and farther out than she expected, but better to avoid the middle of her bottom that was about to receive a spanking, and a safe distance from the sciatic nerve.

I uncapped one of the needles, and said, "Here it is," as I inserted the needle with a quick jab.

Liz groaned a little, but seemed to be learning not to complain.

I then stepped over, and swabbed her left buttock. "This will hurt more, because I'm going to put the needle against your skin, and then push, until it is in. I then did exactly that, seeing her skin indent nearly half an inch before the needle popped through. I slowly pushed it in all the way to the hub.

"Ow! That hurt!"

I laughed, "Good, then it will be punishment that might help you learn to cooperate with me!" Liz groaned again.

I walked back around the desk to my chair and sat down. I looked at Liz, and her face was scrunched-up. "Relax, Liz, the needles are going to be in for a few minutes. Just get used to it."

I then turned to my computer, opened a browser, and paid no attention to Liz. After a few minutes, I quit the browser and looked at Liz. "Do you think you've learned your lesson, now? We cannot start your punishment until you understand how important it is to obey me."

"Oh, yes sir, I understand. I'm sorry. I'll cooperate."

She's learning! "That's better." I smiled.

I walked around the desk to behind Liz, and wiggled each of the needles. Liz groaned, but didn't say anything. "I'm going to make sure you understand." I pulled each of the needles out about ½", and then pushed them both back in at the same time.

"Ow! ... Sorry, Sir!"

"OK. I think you've got the idea. I pulled each of the needles out, and disposed of them in a 'sharps' container that sat on the credenza behind the desk. I then walked around behind Liz, and pulled up her underwear, running my fingers around inside the waistband, to make sure it was smooth. I told Liz that she could stand up and, to my delight, she immediately stood and got into the standing position as I had taught her.

"We are now going to get started on your first level-10 punishment, which will be a bare-bottom hand spanking. I will give you a warm-up on your underwear so that you can get used to the intensity of the spanking. I don't want to have a problem with you and have to give you more corrective punishment."

"Oh, no Sir, I will cooperate."

I smiled. "Very good. Come with me."

We walked to the center of the playroom, and I pulled over the armless chair, grabbing the Ping Pong paddle that was lying on top of it. I sat down, and pointed to my lap, "Liz, get across my lap, now!"

Liz complied immediately, draping herself over me. I adjusted her position so that her toes were barely touching the ground, and both of her hands were flat on the ground. "You must stay in this position throughout your spanking. Do you understand?"

"Yes, Sir," came the reply from near the floor.

"If you get out of position, I will swat you with the paddle; do you understand?"

"Yes, Sir," Liz said resignedly.

"OK, then. You will receive 50 spanks on your underwear as a warm-up. Are you ready?"

Liz adjusted her position a bit, and then answered, "Yes, Sir."

With that, I began spanking her with my open hand, alternating sides, and giving her about one spank every two seconds. This warm-up would take about 2 minutes.

Liz let out a couple of groans and 'Ow!'s', but remained in position. The 50 spanks seemed to take a long time, but I was already thinking of the main punishment – with her underwear down – that would take much longer. At the end of the warm-up spanking, Liz was breathing hard, and fidgeting, but staying pretty well in position.

"Now, your underwear will come down, and I will administer your main punishment." I lowered her underwear, and she helpfully lifted her middle to allow the panties to come down – down her legs, down almost to her knees. I was now staring at Liz' beautiful bare bottom, which was just a bit pink from the warm-up spanking.

"You will now receive 200 hard spanks on your bottom. I'll start out slowly, and increase the speed and intensity up to the end. I want you to request your punishment, and then I will begin."

After a few seconds, Liz said, "Please, Sir, may I have my spanking now?"

Perfect. "Yes, you may!" And I began her bare-bottomed spanking.

I started spanking her at the same rate as before, alternating sides. After about two-dozen spanks, I stopped to ask how she was doing.

"I'm fine, Sir. But the spanking really hurts!"

"I told you it would – that's how it has to be, if this punishment is going to be of any help to you." And I started spanking her again. By the time we were up to about 100 spanks, Liz started whimpering quietly. As I continued spanking her, I said, "It can't be that bad, I'm just using my hand. Wait until we get to the more severe implements!"

Liz sobbed harder. At 173 spanks, Liz could not help herself, and reached back to rub her bottom. I immediately stopped the spanking, carefully twisted her arm behind her back and held it there. I picked up the Ping-Pong paddle, and told Liz, "If you had lifted one hand or foot, I would have given you a light swat on that side. If you had lifted your body up, I would have given you a couple of swats on each side. But you have done exactly what I told you *not* to do: Reach behind, and interfere with the spanking. So you will now receive three swats on each side."

I lifted the paddle, and brought it down with some force on her bare right cheek. Liz yelped, but stayed in position. I continued the paddling, alternating sides, until she had received three swats on each side. Her bottom was starting to really look red, now. I asked Liz, "Can we continue your spanking, now?"

She answered softly, "Yes, Sir."

I finished her spanking with another 27 hard and fast spanks, and had no doubt that my hand hurt as much as her bottom.

Liz was softly sobbing, but I waited and, after about 30 seconds, Liz looked back at me, and said "Thank you, Sir, for my spanking."

I rubbed her bottom, and said "Good girl!" Now, we'll begin your first corner time.

I had planned ahead well, and had already lubed the rectal thermometer, hiding it in a tissue on the small table next to the chair. I reached over, and grabbed it. "Liz, I'm going to insert a rectal thermometer now, and it will remain in you for 5 full minutes."

She sniffled, "Yes sir." I separated her buttocks with both hands, and found her anus; she was obviously clenching her muscles. "Liz, you have to relax your bottom, now. Cooperation means making it easier for me to administer your punishment."

"OK, Sir." She sniffled again.

I held her buttocks apart with my left hand, while inserting the thermometer smoothly into her rectum with my right hand. Liz squealed again, and then giggled.

"Is this funny?" I asked her.

"No Sir, it just feels strange."

I moved the thermometer around in circles, and then slowly pulled it out and plunged it back in. Liz was finally starting to relax her anus, and I continued moving the thermometer around, so that she would be sure to feel it in her.

After a couple of minutes, I let her buttocks go, and left the thermometer in her with an inch or so sticking out. I rubbed Liz' red bottom, and she moaned again.

Then, I realized that my leg was wet – Liz was leaking her sex juices on me, and I realized that she might actually be getting turned on. While I moved the thermometer around a bit with my left hand, I put my right hand between her legs and under her, moving upward over her labia, to her clitoris.

Liz jumped, and I heard a breathless 'Oh!'

I made a 'V' with my fingers, and let them slide along each side of her clit, lifting the hood slightly on each stroke. Liz moaned again, and I could tell that she was progressing nicely in her turned-on state, but I quickly removed my hand. I gave her a slap on each buttock – causing her to jump again, and yell "Ow!"

I laughed, and told her, "Liz, you are here to be punished. If you take your punishment well, I might allow you to come ... but for now, I don't want you getting any closer to having an orgasm. If you have an orgasm before I authorize it, I will begin this punishment again from the beginning."

Liz groaned – not a sexual moan, this time – and said, dejectedly, "Yes Sir, I understand."

The timer on my watch buzzed, and I separated Liz' buttocks again, moved the thermometer around roughly, and then pulled it out. I told her to stand up, and take her underwear off. I walked to the bathroom, and quickly washed the thermometer, leaving it on the counter.

When I re-entered the playroom, Liz was standing next to the chair in the standing position, with her hands on her head. She gave me a slight smile, and I commended her, "Good girl! I was wondering whether you would remember this time, or needed a few more needles in your bottom."

"Oh no, Sir, I don't need that. I am a good girl."

I laughed, "We'll see about that when I give you the next level-10 punishments, which will be much harder than the spanking you just took." Liz' eyes went down to the floor, and her facial cheeks looked as flushed as her butt cheeks looked red.

I went back into the office area, moved the chairs aside, and cleared a few things from the desk. I asked Liz to come over, and she stood in front of the desk.

"Now, please go to the side of the desk. Put your feet outside each leg of the desk, and bend over with your chest fully down on the desk." I watched, while Liz stepped up to the side of the desk, put her feet on either side of the desk legs, and bent over.

I put my hand on her back, and applied gentle pressure, until she was flat on the desk, with her bottom up in the air and her legs separated widely. This was actually the first time I had seen her genitals fully from behind: Her labia looked swollen, and were separated, with the pink of her glistening inner tissues clearly on display.

I was now getting turned-on because I knew Liz was responding to the spanking by getting turned-on herself. The entire experience seemed surreal, but was going very nicely, and according to the script. It was clear that Liz was trying hard to cooperate, and that she was interested in really experiencing some pain.

I walked to the executive chair behind the desk and sat down. I put my head in my hands on the desk, close to Liz, and spoke to her softly. "Liz, I am proud of you! You are taking your punishment very well."

She smiled, "Thank you, Sir."

I continued, "Now, you are graduating to a more intense experience – the tawse."

"Tawz? Never heard of it ... Sir."

"It's a Scottish leather strap with two or three thin tails. It used to be the standard punishment in the boarding schools in Scotland, and other parts of the U.K., during the last century. The one I have is a replica of the original 'Lochlelly' tawse, one of the most feared punishment implements, used on girls as well as boys.

"Here, let me show you." I opened the cabinet behind the desk, and pulled out an 18-inch, 3-tailed leather tawse. It was beautifully crafted, with woven handle in red and black leather. The 'tails' were quite stiff, and drooped only slightly, when I held the tawse horizontally.

"It is similar to the old 'razor strop' – a wide, single-piece heavy leather strap that was used in the U.S. for punishments 'in the woodshed'."

Still bent over flat on the desk, Liz looked at the tawse that lay on the desk front of her, and said, "I don't want to think about it ... just do it."

I told her, "You're a brave girl, and this punishment will do you good." I then decided to draw the tension out a bit more ... so I sat back down in my chair.

"Liz, I need to explain something to you before you receive this next punishment."

"Sir?"

"You can take what I'm saying as part of the role play, or reality – it will be true in both cases. As the one giving the punishment, it is my responsibility to ensure your safety. What we are doing is based on trust: You are trusting me to give you an experience that involves pain – perhaps even up to your limit, but you're also trusting me to not hurt you seriously. Not hurting you is my first priority – I don't want to do anything that would require medical attention, or make any marks that won't be gone in a few weeks, at worst." After that exaggeration, I couldn't keep a straight face, and my smile showed through my stern exterior countenance.

Liz looked at me questioningly, then frowned, and looked down at the desk.

I turned serious again. "If you have never received a serious corporal punishment before, you are going to think that you can't take the pain; that I'm damaging your bottom; or that you might even pass out. But I am watching you carefully, and will make sure that I don't exceed your 'real' limits – which are undoubtedly much higher than you realize."

Liz was still looking down, with her eyes closed. I continued, "Every few strokes, I will rub your bottom. That isn't (just) for my enjoyment, but to help distribute the pain, so you can take more, and so that I can feel your skin, and determine whether more strokes with a certain implement will cause damage. I am very careful: The last thing I want is to actually hurt you – other than giving your bottom some pain that will wear off in a matter of hours, and some redness, soreness, and possibly light bruising, that will fade within a few days."

I'm not sure if this made Liz more comfortable, to know that I was punishing her carefully, or more uncomfortable, to know that her next punishments would be more serious. Liz finally said, "I understand, Sir. I appreciate that you're taking care of me."

"Liz, this brings up another point, that may help explain what turns me on about all this. We are all defensive, and protective against receiving pain. But if you are willing to accept a certain amount of pain, that demonstrates both control of your mind over your body, and trust that the pain will be given in a challenging way, but not be too severe. It is the combination of openness and trust that is the real turn-on for me."

I stood up, picked up the tawse, and walked around behind Liz. I took a few moments to admire her body – especially her now-reddened bottom, and the now-moist private parts peeking out from below. Suddenly, I had another thought; something that I had not fantasized about before.

"We're going to do your second level-10 punishment a bit differently. I am going to insert a small butt plug now, and you will hold that in throughout your tawsing."

Liz looked back at me, as I lubed the small butt plug, and then faced forward shaking her head.

I told her, "Please reach back and hold your buttocks apart for me."

Liz did as instructed, and I moved the butt plug around her anus, and then slowly inserted it, until its neck held it in place. I told her, "OK – get back down. I will now administer 18 strokes of the tawse."

Liz let go of her buttocks, and placed her hands in front of her on the desk. She swayed back and forth, and finally settled into a firm stance. I then instructed her: "Say 'Ready!' when you are ready for a stroke of the tawse, and then give me the count, and a 'Thank you, Sir' after each stroke. Do you understand?"

Liz barely managed to croak out a 'Yes, Sir' as I placed the tawse against her bare bottom, ready to begin her second level-10 punishment.

After about 30 seconds, I said, "I'm waiting ...".

A few seconds later, Liz said, "Ready!"

I pulled the tawse back, and swung it quickly towards her buttocks. WHAP! It struck mainly on her left side, but wrapped around to the right cheek, creating a dark red stripe.

About a second later, Liz yelled, "One, thank you, Sir!"

I placed the tawse against her bottom again, and waited. "Ready!" she called out. Again, I swung the tawse at full force, and it struck her bottom with a loud CRACK! Almost immediately, she screamed, "Two, thank you, Sir."

We continued the tawsing, with Liz obediently calling out 'ready' and 'thank you' for each stroke. By stroke 8, she was sobbing again, and the time between the 'thank you, sir' and the next 'ready' grew longer, eventually taking nearly a minute.

But Liz bravely continued on, calling out 'Ready!' after which I would give her a hard stroke of the heavy leather implement, and she would cry, breathe hard, and then give me the count and a 'Thank you, Sir'.

The tawsing took nearly 10 minutes, and Liz was in tears, as she held each side of the desk tightly with her hands, her very red bottom quivering uncontrollably. Although she lifted a foot or a hand a few times, I didn't make her take a corrective punishment.

When the tawsing was over, Liz remained in position, softly weeping.

I told her, "Now, you're going to learn the 'chair' position." I pulled one of the chairs back in front of the desk, and turned it around. Liz climbed into it, with her knees against the arms, about halfway back on the chair.

"Get your bottom up, Liz! Head down on the back of the chair!" I then held the butt plug, and told Liz to give a small push. The butt plug came out, and I set it aside on a tissue.

I walked around to the cabinet above the desk, and pulled out a beautiful butt plug, with glass spheres of increasing diameter along the body of the plug. I showed it to Liz, and then walked around behind her, and took my time lubing the device. I then set it against her anus, and pushed gently, until it moved into her, each sphere dilating her anus then popping in, giving her a very unique feeling.

I heard a few 'Oooh!'s' and moans from Liz, but she took the insertion well.

I moved the butt plug in and out of her, while she kept her position in the chair. Eventually, I slid it all the way in, walked around the desk, and sat back down in my chair. I looked at her red, teary eyes, and said, "Well, you've completed level 20 out of 50!"

She groaned, knowing well that what was to come would be much worse than what had come before.

I played with the papers on my desk, and finally said to her, "Liz, since you've behaved so well, I will offer you – this time only – a substitute for one of your level 10 punishments. Instead of the school paddle or the birch, I will offer you a substitute punishment of some shots in your bottom. I will give them simultaneously, and they will stay in you for 2-3 minutes. We'll keep the butt plug in, until your shots are finished. Would you like to take that substitute, or shall I get the 'board' (a large paddle, ½-inch thick and 18 inches long)?"

Liz groaned, and said, "OK, Sir. I'll take the shots."

"Good choice, Liz. For these, I'll let you get comfortable, and lie down. Come with me." Liz got up slowly, the bumpy glass butt plug reminding her that she was still being punished. We walked to the back of the room, and I pulled the drapes, exposing the large bed.

Liz looked at me quizzically, but I told her sternly to lie face down on the bed, and wait for her shots. I then went back to my desk to assemble the syringes and needles. I decided to give her 6 cc, in two injections, on each side.

When the shots were ready, I carried them to the bed, and put them on the nightstand. I lay down next to Liz, and lightly rubbed her back, while I spoke with her. "How are you doing, Liz?"

She turned her head, and looked at me. "I'm not sure I can take even another level-10 punishment; my bottom is already very sore."

I smiled at her, and said, "Let's get your shots started, and we can continue our conversation."

I stood up, walked to the side of the bed and retrieved the shots and an alcohol swab. I swabbed her right buttock with alcohol, and inserted the needle. Liz flinched a little when the needle went in, but was otherwise silent. I injected 3 cc, and she groaned again. Leaving the first needle in, I swabbed her left buttock, and inserted the other needle, and injected 3 cc on that side, also.

I put my face down near Liz, and ran my fingers through her hair. "This is your third level-10 punishment. I'm going to leave these shots in for a couple more minutes, and then give you two more." I rubbed her back, and marveled that Liz was in my playroom, her bare bottom exposed, a butt plug in her rectum, and a shot being given on each side. I knew that this wasn't what she had expected, but she didn't complain.

After a couple of minutes, I removed the needle from her right side, and re-inserted it several inches higher up and farther to the side. I slowly injected the last 3 cc, while keeping my left hand on her bottom. Then, I pulled out the needle from her left side, and gave her another shot higher up on that side, as well. Liz moaned a little.

After another two minutes, I pulled out the needles, and disposed of the shots. Liz stayed in position on the bed. When I returned, I told her to get into a knee-chest position. She did so, and I pulled the glass butt plug out of its position, and moved it in and out of her slowly. Finally, I took it out completely, and told Liz that she could stand up. She immediately got off the bed, and into in the standing position, awaiting my next instructions.

I walked into the bathroom next door and, after washing the butt plug and leaving it on the counter, I took a large wooden hairbrush from the drawer. I entered the playroom, walked over to where Liz was standing, and softly told her, "It's time for your fourth level-10 punishment."

Liz groaned again, and finally said, "Yes, Sir."

I smiled at her and said, "I'm going to undress you now for the rest of your punishment."

Liz stood still as I walked around in back of her. I unclipped the hem of her dress on both sides, and let it fall. I walked back in front of her and slowly scanned from head to toe: Liz was barefoot, but wearing the dress and – except for the redness of her eyes – looked ready to go to a party; of course, I knew that she wasn't wearing underwear, and that the dress was hiding a very red bottom.

I stepped up to her, and hugged her. My hand dropped to cradle her bottom, causing her to jump slightly and say, "Ow! My butt really is going to be sore for a while!" I kissed her on the cheek, and then walked behind her.

I unzipped Liz' dress and, as I took it off her shoulders, Liz took her hands from her head long enough for me to slip the sleeves off, and drop the dress to the ground. I unhooked her bra, and Liz again brought her hands down so that I could slip it off. I reached down and picked up her things and casually walked over to one of the desk chairs, where I put down her bra and underwear and hung her dress over the back.

I returned to Liz, who remained in the standing position near the front of the bed. I took in her beauty – from her long legs, curvaceous hips and bottom, to her small but shapely breasts. By the time my eyes arrived at her face, she was smiling at me, and asked, "Do you like what you see?" Of course, I had seen Liz nude many times, but in this situation she looked vulnerable, and – somehow – even more beautiful.

I put one of the pillows on the bedspread to my left, sat down on the bed, and told Liz to stand between my legs, and then to lie across my left thigh. As she maneuvered into position, with her breasts up against the outside of my left leg and her head on the pillow, I had no doubt that she could feel my erection pushing against her, but she didn't say anything. I clamped my right leg over her legs, to prevent any possibility of her kicking or bucking. Then, I took the hairbrush, and laid it on Liz' left buttock.

"Liz, this is going to be a quick and hard hair-brushing. If you stay in position, and take your punishment, it will be over in less than two minutes. But it's going to hurt, and you can expect to see bruises for a few days." Liz didn't say anything, but I saw a ripple of fear pass through her body.

I tightened my right leg over her legs, to make sure she stayed in position, and told her, "You may request your punishment, now."

Liz swallowed hard, and said, "May I please have my hair-brushing now?"

I said, "Yes, you may," and began striking her with the hairbrush, alternating sides, and leaving dark red marks after each stroke.

Liz was breathing hard, and sobbing, but held her position. I expected her to say 'Please' or 'No more', but she took her punishment without comment or complaint. I was a bit hard on her, giving her a real hair-brushing that undoubtedly would make it difficult for her to sit down for several days.

When her hair-brushing was done, Liz was sobbing quietly, and I lifted my right leg from her legs, and pulled her onto my lap. I slipped my right hand between her legs, and under her, sliding up to stroke her clit. Her sobbing quieted, but her breathing became even more ragged.

I said, "Liz, you're almost finished with your punishment, and I will allow you to have an orgasm now, if you like." She just nodded her head, and buried it in the pillow.

I stroked her, and swirled my fingers around her clit. The animalistic sounds coming from Liz began to morph, from groans of pain to moans of pleasure. Liz rocked back and forth across my lap, as I continued stroking her.

"Liz, I'm going to insert the small vibrator as your corner time, while we do this."

All I heard from her was a quiet "Umm hmm."

I reached over to the bedside dresser, and picked up the already-lubed vibrator that was an inch in diameter and about seven inches long, looking mean in pure black. I stopped stroking so that I could insert the vibrator, separating Liz' buttocks with my left hand. Liz moaned again and her anal muscles tightened, when she felt the tip of the vibrator.

"Just relax," I said, as I moved the tip slightly in and out, going a bit further in with each stroke.

Liz relaxed her sphincter, and the vibrator slid into her rectum until there was less than two inches sticking out of her.

I resumed stroking Liz underneath while I wiggled the vibrator with my left hand, resting my left arm on Liz' bottom. With my right hand, I splayed my fingers (briefly visualizing the Vulcan salute), and advanced them around Liz' clit, moving up and back, while I progressively tightened my fingers and applied more pressure, gently squeezing her clit with each advance.

At the same time, my left hand began moving the vibrator in and out, gradually at first, but moving farther with each stroke – never coming fully out of her, but moving over a three or four inch range, sliding easily through her well-lubed anus. As I looked down to my left at her bare back and head nearly hidden by her blond hair, I could see that Liz was rocking, and she was emitting a continuous, very low, moan – almost like a cat purring.

I quickened the pace of my strokes and then, as my hand slid up and the vibrator went in, I suddenly squeezed my fingers around her clit, and moved the vibrator in rapid circles, as I held it deep in her.

Liz inhaled quickly, and as I moved my hand down and then back up, my thumb entered her deeply, as my middle fingers surrounded her clit, squeezing again gently. Liz' body suddenly stiffened, she threw her head back, and a shrill tone came from her throat. Her middle bucked up and down, as she came, and then came some more as I brought my hand back, and then advanced it with two fingers entering her wet grotto.

I curled my fingers and put pressure on her anterior vaginal wall – her 'G-spot', as I felt her squeeze her sexual secretions like a thick cream over my fingers. With my left hand, I slowly pulled the vibrator out of her bottom.

Liz and I were still for a while – my fingers still deep in her, her back rising and falling as she panted heavily. I slid my fingers out of her, and rested both of my forearms on her bottom, waiting for Liz to return to a more-normal breathing pattern.

"You may get up when you're ready," I whispered.

She tilted her head on the bed, looking back at me, with a smile on her face, cheeks red, and a slight 'aura' surrounding her. "Do I have to get up?" she replied, with a quick chuckle.

"You may stay there for a few more minutes. At least I'm glad that you can laugh, after all the punishment you've taken."

Liz didn't comment, and I slowly rubbed her bottom, circling the tender skin of each of her buttocks. We were quiet again for several minutes, and then Liz said, "OK. I guess I'm ready." She slid off my lap, and stood up, flashing a brief smile at me, and then getting immediately into the standing position.

"Liz, you really have learned how to behave yourself ... at least with me. Perhaps this punishment will motivate you to treat your husband better?"

Liz looked at me and frowned, "You sure know how turn me on ... and off!"

I laughed, "Well, sorry, but I need to get you into the proper frame of mind to take your last level-10 punishment."

Liz groaned, "I guess we have to?"

"Yes, Liz – we have a punishment plan, and I will not disappoint you." I saw her eyes sparkle at that, and for once she seemed to have a loss for words.

I sat on the bed, looking at Liz standing there obediently. I realized that she would, of course, take whatever punishment I dished out. She had taken her spankings well so far, and submitted to everything that I had done to her, without complaint. My heart softened, and I decided to reward her for her performance thus far.

"I was planning for your last level-10 punishment to be a caning. And a level-10 caning would be 12 strokes of the school cane." I walked over to a cabinet, and pulled out a cane, and flexed it, as I slowly walked back to Liz. "This is the school cane. It is a pretty severe implement." It was ¼" in diameter, and intended to bruise – much too heavy of an implement for today's 'punishment'.

Liz' mouth dropped open, and I could see tears coming to her eyes. I slowly walked back to the cabinet, hanging the school cane back up, and pulled out a much thinner cane. Again I walked back to where Liz was standing, and put the cane on the bed. I paced slowly back and forth in front of Liz, who stood there naked and silent.

Finally, I stopped in front of her, and said, "I have some good news and bad news for you ..."

Liz looked at me hopefully, and said, "I'll take the good news."

I returned her look, and said, "You'll take whatever news I give you, young lady!" Then my serious face softened, and I laughed. Promisingly, Liz laughed also, but in a restrained way. She quieted and waited for my pronouncement.

"First, some good news. Liz, after consideration of how well you have taken your punishment to this point, I have decided to give you another substitute for part of your last level-10 punishment. Instead of the school cane, I will use this very thin cane; it will sting like hell, but it won't bruise like the thicker cane. Also, I will administer only a level-5 caning, which will be 6 strokes."

Liz seemed to relax a little, and I told her, "You may put your hands on your hips." I knew that Liz was getting tired with her hands on her head, and I wanted her to save all of her strength for the punishment that was coming.

Liz waited for the other shoe to drop ... "The bad news is, you will need to take your caning 'free-standing'."

"What is that?" Liz asked.

"I'm going to have you bend over and hold your ankles. You will be responsible for getting back into position after each stroke."

"Uh ... OK."

"And, we're going to have to decide on your last level-5 punishment." Liz groaned again. I picked up the cane from the bed, and turned toward Liz, "please spread your legs 6" wider, and bend over and hold your ankles."

Liz did as she was told, but when she tried to reach her ankles, she remarked, "I can't really do this, and keep my legs straight."

I said, "That's OK. You may bend your knees."

I walked around Liz, so that I was standing behind her, and to her left. I said, simply, "Bend!"

Liz bent further down, grabbing her ankles, and thrusting her bottom into the air. By this time, there was no issue of embarrassment, and Liz relaxed, with her anus wide open, and her buttocks ready for the next punishment.

I placed the thin cane across her bottom, and took my time, sliding it back and forth across her buttocks, as a knife cutting through a wedding cake. Suddenly, I brought the cane back, and then forward – slicing through the air, and landing on Liz' bottom with incredible force – sounding like a 'CRACK!' and sending ripples through her buttocks and down her legs.

"Aiyeeeee!!! That really hurt!" she yelled.

Although – as expected – Liz let go of her ankles and rose up about halfway, she quickly bent back down, and grabbed her ankles.

I said, "Yes – it's supposed to hurt!"

Liz wept softly, as I repositioned the cane across her already-red bottom. Again, the cane was pulled back, and swung firmly across her bottom, making another loud 'CRACK!' and causing Liz to let go of her ankles and sway back and forth. Liz smartly did not grab her bottom, as she was so inclined to do, but bent back over and reached again for her ankles.

"Very good!" I said. "You have four more coming ..."

Liz held her position, as I waited, watching her bottom quiver. Once again, I quickly brought the cane back, and swung it with force – and a wrist snap at the end –

crashing it loudly onto her bottom. A loud 'CRACK!!' echoed throughout the room.

Liz lifted up, and I quickly said, "Down! Right now!"

Liz complied, and bent over again.

I brought the cane back, and waited ... watching Liz' buttocks sway and quiver, anticipating the next stroke. Without warning, I brought the cane down on her swollen buttocks with a 'SMACK!!!'.

Liz shrieked, and began crying for real. I rubbed her bottom with my right hand, and confirmed that although the cane strokes were stinging her, they were not leaving raised welts on her bottom.

I administered the last two strokes with Liz in tears, the final stroke falling where her upper thighs and buttocks joined. She remained in position, even after the sound of the last stroke had died down.

Liz was sobbing softly, and I put my hand under her, and slowly moved it back and forth over her genital area. Finally, I told Liz to stand up, and she assumed the standing position, eyes red, and tears streaming down her cheeks.

I asked her, "What do you have to say?"

Amazingly, and reassuringly, Liz said, "Thank you, Sir!"

We hugged – her naked and trembling, and I with a huge erection pushing at my pants; I was very impressed and pleased that Liz could complete her punishment voluntarily.

Liz sniffled as I reached my hands around her, and held her bottom. I rubbed her buttocks, as I kissed her neck, and then I began to cry myself. Liz tensed momentarily, and looked up at me with puffy, red eyes. "Thank you, Sir, for the punishment," she said softly. She made a move to kiss me, but I averted my head, and we put our cheeks together, and held each other tightly.

I then let go of Liz, and took a step back. "Standing position!" I commanded. Liz faithfully took the standing position, looking at me with a sense of curiosity, but I felt her trust and complete abandonment, as I looked into her eyes, and we had a 'together' moment.

I lifted Liz' head with my thumb under her chin, and asked, "Would you like to take the final level-5 punishment now, or come back sometime in the next week, when your bottom is feeling better?"

Liz looked up at me with big brown eyes, and said, "I'd like to come back for the rest of my punishment, Sir." That was probably the most rewarding – and exciting – thing that happened during Liz' punishment.

We took a quick shower together, and Liz bent over the desk one more time, so that I could rub a soothing lotion on her bottom. She stood up, turning around to face me, and suddenly hugged me tightly. She began crying, and we held each other for a long time.

I handed Liz her underwear, then her bra, and finally her dress, and she quietly got dressed. We held each other, and I kissed her on her nose. We hugged once more, and I held her bottom and pulled her close to me.

Liz did come back several days later for her remaining punishment, which was uneventful, but still very satisfying. Liz had submitted to a very hard thrashing of her bottom, while cooperating completely, and taking an amount of pain that she did not think was possible. The punishment didn't make much immediate difference in how she treated her husband, but Liz and her husband reconciled somewhat.

Liz and I had a close relationship after that, but over the next few months, she became more family-focused, and less willing to indulge my fantasies. We exercised together and she was still casual about changing in front of me, but we never again had a 'close encounter of the spanking kind'. I had hoped to play doctor with Liz, and offered a few times to 'relieve her pain' with an intramuscular injection ... but she wasn't turned-on by this aspect of my fantasy, and eventually I stopped asking.

Less than a year after our role-play, Liz' husband was transferred overseas, and they moved away from the neighborhood, and out of my life. I will always fondly remember Liz and the time I spent with her, especially the day I satisfied the requirements of the pink punishment note that she had given me.

CHAPTER 7: ALL DRESSED UP, NOWHERE TO GO

After Liz' punishment, my spanking fantasies grew, rather than diminished. I replayed the experience many times in my head. A single 'scene' was sufficient to get me off, but with each re-imagining I embellished and re-molded what had actually occurred into new, more exciting, fantasies.

If only I had thought of some of these things before the experience with Liz! If only I had another chance to act out my fully developed fantasy in real life. But I thought it unlikely that I would find another willing punishment partner anytime soon.

My new fantasies called for new spanking implements and additional supplies, which I ordered via the Internet. I re-arranged the furniture in the playroom, and added a few key items, which further advanced my fantasies.

I was in a positive feedback loop – fantasizing about new things, and then equipping my playroom so that these could be acted out, which led to additional fantasies and more new toys. My collection now included whips, floggers, and leather paddles, as well as some ordinary household items that could be put to good use on some young woman's behind ... providing that I ever found a young (or older) woman willing to play with me.

I considered advertising in Craig's List for a submissive who wanted to try some new experiences, and wrote several ads (leading to more fantasies), but could never bring myself to actually place any of them. It just seemed too dangerous – inviting a strange woman into my home, and doing things that – if misunderstood – could lead to a lawsuit.

I drafted several versions of a 'punishment agreement' that would need to be signed before I would feel comfortable playing with a stranger. If you had asked me, I would have admitted that I never expected to actually have an opportunity to use any of these agreements, but it was a turn-on writing them, and imagining how I would present such an agreement to a nervous young woman. While the first versions of these agreements were focused on protecting me legally, they evolved into a short list of rules that I would expect a punishment partner (the 'bottom') to obey, my responsibilities as 'top', and a short list of things that partner could expect during the spanking experience.

After the playroom was made ready to support any of my fantasies – assuming I could find a willing female partner – I turned my attention to the spare bedroom in the basement. Driven by some of my more recent fantasies, I converted the bedroom to a medical 'exam' room, complete with rolling IV stands, a shelf of instruments, and a cabinet with supplies. As in the playroom, I installed several hidden video cameras with great angles on where my "patients" would be, to record the action ... if there were ever any patients. In contrast to the playroom, however, the medical exam room was brightly lit – creating a very different atmosphere.

My Internet shopping sprees tracked my browsing of porn sites, which had morphed from pure spanking to BDSM, needle play, enemas and medical sex. I bought an exam table, complete with stirrups, from a used medical equipment supply house. After installing some cabinets and a small sink (running the plumbing under the house from the bathroom across the hall), the exam table took up most of the room.

I bought dozens of small items that made the exam room more realistic, including a wall-mounted "sharps" container, blood pressure instrument ("sphygmo-manometer"), and otoscope kit. I bought a large glass jar with wide top, and several ancient glass syringes. And I kept a bottle of formaldehyde with which I could soak a sponge to make the exam room smell like a real old-fashioned doctor's office.

My fantasies evolved, as I surfed the web, and my shopping followed by stocking-up on the supplies that would be required for each fantasy: acupuncture needles, catheters, hospital gowns and surgical scrubs, a roll of the waxy paper used on the exam table, and under-pads for wet play.

I went through a phase of purchasing various medical instruments, from a variety of specula for gynecologic exams, to a couple of real endoscopes, including a colonoscope that was nearly four feet long (very intimidating to a patient sitting on the exam table, even if never to actually be used).

Driven by more exploration on the web, I became fascinated by the thought of giving enemas. I hung enema bags from the IV pole in the exam room, and assembled a collection of specialized enema tubes and nozzles. I had balloon catheters used for retention enemas, and long tubes used for administering colonics. I bought several metal enema nozzles that were similar to the butt plugs, but with holes at the tip for spraying water in various patterns, and a connector that was used to hook-up the enema tubing. I gave myself one enema, which I didn't like very much, although I managed to move he nozzle around enough to stimulate my prostate.

I also bought some very large syringes that could be used to quickly inject 200cc (6 ounces) of water into the rectum. I augmented these with several bulb syringes (much larger versions of the bulbs used for ear cleaning), and even a turkey baster.

With the acquisition of each piece of equipment, my fantasies evolved. I had become an expert at masturbating, but after a lifetime being with someone I loved, I was lonely and bored. It was disheartening to think that with all of my toys, and perfect set-up for role-play, I would probably never actually have someone with whom to share my fantasies.

I wasn't a hermit, living in my man-cave, however. Several of my friends were intent on setting me up with 'dates' – mostly older women (i.e., my age), who were very nice. But, I could not envision playing with any of them, and was never brave enough to share my fantasies – especially since most of them were friends-of-friends, and I couldn't take the chance that my closest friends would find out about my fetish-filled fantasy world.

None of these relationships advanced to the point of having sex, and I could not imagine how any of these women would have reacted, had I shared what I was thinking while I was with them, or – God forbid – brought them into my medical exam room. I took some weekend trips with a few of my female friends – a few involving a lot of intimate hugging, but most others just capitalizing on a friendship that was open and trusting enough to share a room, and even a bed.

Most of these women became close and long-lasting friends. I did bring up the general subject of fantasies with some of them, and a few were open enough to share their fantasies. Some were at least as bizarre as mine: Being gang-raped in the back of a pickup truck by a dozen black men, for example. But none involved either spanking or medical procedures – or, for that matter, any form of submission.

I invited a couple of my closer women friends to surf the web with me, strategically passing through some of my favorite spanking sites, but the images were shocking to these women, and I received no offers to play, or even indications of interest.

Most of these women were very 'mature' - they had been married, or had other long-term relationships, and many life experiences. They were comfortable with their bodies (although not necessarily with the aging process), and – as I dated mainly liberal women – many had gone for years to nude beaches, had experienced many medical procedures (about a third had undergone hysterectomies, and nearly two thirds had at least a little urinary incontinence); they had spanked their kids, and played with many sexual partners.

Actually, they would have been very safe sex partners: They almost certainly did not have an STD; some were already into menopause, making pregnancy a non-issue (of course, my vasectomy would take care of that); and their maturity and realistic outlook minimized the chances of emotional tie-ups. But they weren't a turn-on to me.

I realized that much of the 'excitement' of my fantasies was in introducing women to new things, and having them 'submit' to things that might be frightening or embarrassing to them. But the women that I was seeing were mature and experienced, while my fantasies were still rooted in my childhood – things that had been frightening or embarrassing to me, especially in my pre-adolescent years: Being seen undressed, getting spanked, or being taken to the doctor to get shots.

What I needed, in order to really live my fantasies, was a younger woman who would be excited by the 'new' things to which I exposed her; someone who just wanted to hang-out and play, without committing to a deep relationship; or someone already in a relationship, who might want to safely explore a few 'forbidden' fantasies.

But most younger women typically have other, more romantic, interests: More often than not, they want a meaningful and loving relationship that might lead to marriage and children.

Furthermore, young women have plenty of friends their own age, and have no need for an older man – other than as a possible father figure (ouch!). Most young women would probably not be mature enough to accept and see past the pain; and they would be too independent to agree to submit to anyone else – especially someone who reminded them of the submission to their parents in the not-so-distant past.

It has been claimed that people who are turned-on by spanking were abused during their youth, but this has not been my experience – either personally, or among the women with whom I've broached the subject. Those who were 'abused' (with corporal punishment used regularly in the household) are now generally totally against spanking, or hitting of any kind. They cannot imagine how anyone could be turned-on by something as degrading and primitive as spanking.

It is those women who were threatened by spanking at home or at school – or observed a friend or relative being spanked, but were never beaten themselves – who may be intrigued by the idea of submitting to a spanking, and see it as a turn-on, even if some pain must be accepted. But it requires a certain maturity to take a sensual spanking – the ability to control your own body, to trust your partner implicitly, and to think beyond the romantic concept of sex to experiences that could be a turn-on, but not lead to love, long-term relationships or procreation.

My thought process evolved over the next year. First was the realization that my fantasies would be a turn-on mainly when acted out with younger women. To whom I could provide new experiences. And for whom submission would be a real challenge – one to which they would need to bring inner strength and youthful openness, while having the maturity to see domination by a partner not as bullying or control, but as an intense freeing of their own psyche. Giving themselves to another person, facing and overcoming inner fears, and eventually abandoning all fear and embarrassment, attaining a relaxed state and new level of consciousness.

Well, that was the idea, anyway. I tried to fantasize about younger women, but always envisioned the old-fashioned schoolgirl who I had seen on television so many years earlier. My mind's eye saw wholesome college girls, in sweaters, carrying their books to class, and I just couldn't find a persona to be the fantasy partner of my daily masturbation; let alone 'real' role-play. I still dated older women occasionally, but avoided any discussion of my fantasies, and saw those women only as close friends, and not fantasy partners.

This was getting frustrating: Now, I could not seem to get turned-on by either older or younger women! Not only was my sex life on a low burner; now my fantasy life was going down the tubes.

I had a great place to play, and lots of toys ... but nobody to play with – or even a vision of how this would ever be more than wasted space in my basement. I could have been building model airplanes or playing golf like most retired men. I thought briefly of emptying the playroom and exam room, and even selling the house. Maybe a condo with a nice swimming pool would give me more of an opportunity to meet women?

Little did I realize that my life was soon going to change: My fantasies would be fulfilled far beyond what I could have ever dreamed ...

###

Thank you for reading Book 1 of the Experiences series. If you enjoyed it, please take a moment to leave a review at your favorite retailer. And, if you liked this story, you'll LOVE the continuation in Book 2: First Experience!

- Simone Freier

Discover other titles by Simone Freier:

Experiences Book 1: Origins of a Fetish

Experiences Book 2: First Experience

Connect with the Author:

Follow me on Twitter: http://twitter.com/SimoneFreier

Friend me on Facebook: http://facebook.com/SimoneFreierAuthor

Visit my Website: http://SimoneFreier.com

Favorite me at Smashwords: http://smashwords.com/SimoneFreier